CHOOSE YOUR PATH BASEBALL BOOK

Out at Home

by
Lisa M. Bolt Simons

Minneapolis, Minnesota

Dedication

To Jana K. and Scott R., I totally appreciate your baseball fanaticism, and thanks for making me laugh so incredibly hard.

Acknowledgements

Thank you to Scott H., Alex D., and Andy L. for your baseball expertise.

Edited by Ryan Jacobson
Game design and "How to Use This Book" by Ryan Jacobson
Cover art by Stephen Morrow

Author photo by Jillian Raye Photography. The following images used under license from Shutterstock.com: bikeriderlondon (promotional photograph), BlueRingMedia (baseball field), KoQ Creative (baseball), and MSF (baseball player)

10 9 8 7 6 5 4 3 2 1

Copyright 2016 by Lisa M. Bolt Simons
Published by Lake 7 Creative, LLC
Minneapolis, MN 55412
www.lake7creative.com

ISBN: 978-1-940647-18-0; eISBN: 978-1-940647-19-7

Table of Contents

How to Use This Book

As you read *Out at Home*, your goal is simple: make it to the happy ending on page 156. It's not as easy as it sounds. You will sometimes be asked to jump to a distant page. Please follow these instructions. Sometimes you will be asked to choose between two or more options. Decide which you feel is best, and go to the corresponding page. (Be careful; some options will lead to disaster.) Finally, if a page offers no instructions or choices, simply continue to the next page.

EARN POINTS

Along the way, you will sometimes collect points for your decisions. Points are awarded for

A) confidence,
B) skill,
C) speed, and
D) teamwork.

Keep track of your points using a bookmark that you can cut out on page 159 (or on a separate piece of paper). You'll need the points later on.

TALENT SCORE

Before you begin, you must determine your talent score. This number stands for the natural ability that your character, Alec, was born with. The number will not change during the story. You can get your talent score in one of three ways:

Quick Way: Give yourself a talent score of two.

Standard Way: If you have any dice, roll one die. The number that you roll is your talent score. (You only get one try. So if you roll a one, you're stuck with it.)

Fun Way: Get a parent or guardian's help (to make sure you're in a safe place where no one—and nothing—can be hurt or damaged). Find a partner to play catch with you. Stand 20 steps apart. Gently toss a rubber ball back and forth six times. This gives you six tries to catch the ball. Every time you catch it, you get a point. You only get six tries, whether the throws are on target or not. If you miss all six, that's okay. As long as you're a good sport and don't get mad, give yourself one talent point for trying the *Fun Way*. Give yourself one skill point, too. After all, skill gets better with practice.

Your Starting Team

GABRIEL NIEVES
left field

ALEC GIBBSEN
shortstop (you)

LANDON KAYYE
third base

JULIAN MENDOZA
center field

ABDI AHMED
right field

ASHTON CATES
second base

LOGAN HANSON
pitcher

WYATT PUFFDON
first base

BEN METEER
catcher

$\mathcal{P}$rologue

*Author's note: Do you have your talent
points yet? If not, please read pages 4–5.*

Bases loaded. You're up next, after Ashton. In your
head, you keep telling yourself, *No pressure. No pressure.
It's only the state quarterfinals.* You practice your swing.

The team is down by two runs, but you can still win
this. What a way to celebrate the end of summer!

But, then, that little voice inside your head becomes
a scream: *It's the bottom of the ninth, two outs, and your
team is down by two runs!*

You swing again, pretending to smack that annoying
voice out of your head and over the fence.

"Come on, Ashton!" you yell toward the batter's box.
"Hit it where they ain't!" It's one of your favorite baseball expressions: hit the ball to a spot where there aren't
any defenders to catch it.

Ashton swings and misses a couple of times. But he also watches three pitches pass wide of the strike zone. That means a full count: three balls and two strikes. One more ball, he gets a walk to first base. One more strike, he's out—and your team, the Cardinals, loses.

You close your eyes briefly. You practice your swing and imagine the bat hitting the ball. If Ashton gets on base, the fate of the season falls to you.

You breathe deep. *Come on, Ashton. Come on.* You don't want to lose.

"Ball four!" the umpire yells.

Yes! You start to jump for joy, but, of course, you stop yourself. There's still work to do. You watch Ashton move to first. All the other runners advance one base, too. That includes Julian, who jogs home and steps on the plate. You high-five him as he runs past.

Now the Cardinals are only down by one.

You're up—with a chance to tie the game . . . or win it . . . or end the season early.

You step into the batter's box and take a couple more warm-up swings. That little voice tries to get back into your head. You push it away from the part of your brain that's saying, *You can do this.*

You hear your friends, teammates, and coaches on the bench, cheering you on.

As you wait for the first pitch, you notice that the third baseman is playing too far back. There's a lot of room in front of him. If you bunt the ball toward him, he won't be able to get it in time to throw you out at first. On the other hand, you're a pretty good hitter. If you swing hard and hit the baseball to the outfield, you could win the game instead of just tie it. What will you choose to do?

To bunt the ball, go to page 42.

To swing away, go to page 29.

"That was a bad idea, August!" you yell.

You don't care that he's a third grader. You spin him around and spank him with all of your strength. The moment your hand makes contact, you know that it was too hard. You hear a loud *thwack*, and your hand starts to sting. If it hurt you that much, you can only imagine what it felt like to him.

August falls to his knees, crying. No, not crying, he's shrieking. The piercing noise fills the house.

Gretchen's voice booms from the bottom of the stairs. "Boys! What on earth is going on?"

"Alec hit me!" cries August.

"He hit me first!" you say, pointing at August.

"Alec, you're old enough to know better," she snaps, and you can hear sadness in her voice. "Oh, Alec, I'm going to have to report this. The policy of our foster home is zero tolerance for violence. I'm afraid . . ."

She covers her mouth. She doesn't finish her sentence. Tears form in her eyes as she hurries out of the room.

Go to the next page.

11

An hour later, you and your brothers are in a car, leaving Chane Valley. You're on your way to a foster home in a different town. You tried to be more grown up. You tried to do the right thing. Now, there are no more families in Chane Valley that can take you. You wonder if you'll ever see your baseball team again.

Go to page 75.

What does he want? To apologize for the umpteenth time? All you can do is groan as you stand.

"I'll wait in here and give you two a minute," says Gretchen. "I didn't get Andy and August, yet. Just let me know when."

"Count to ten."

Gretchen gives you a stern look.

"Fine. Count to sixty."

When you reach the door, your dad grabs you and hugs you.

"What are you doing?" you snap, pushing him away.

"I need to explain some things." He gently ushers you out the door and onto the front stoop. To your surprise, he holds up a couple of baseball gloves. "How about a game of catch—like we used to do?"

You don't have time for this. If you agree to play catch with him, you might not be able to finish your homework. But he is your dad. Maybe you should do as he asks. What will you choose to do?

To play catch, go to page 52.

To just talk, go to page 33.

"Yes," you tell your little brother. "I do love them. They're like peaches and cream."

"Peaches and cream? What does that mean?"

"It means I love them so, so, so much."

"I want to go home," Andy says.

"I think we will soon enough."

 AWARD YOURSELF 1 TEAMWORK POINT.

Go to page 56.

You can't help it; you start to cry. Mrs. Rogers pats your back. Sobs form in your belly and then bark from your mouth.

"I just wish my family was normal," you say.

"If you want, I can give you this notebook," says Mrs. Rogers. She holds it up to show you; it looks new. "You can write how you're feeling, and I can write back."

"Who else would see it?" you ask.

She smiles. "No one else, if that's what you want. But I do have to be honest. If you write about something that's unsafe, I'll have to show the social worker. We want you to be safe in your foster family."

You nod.

"Okay, good. Stay out here as long as you need to." She hands you the notebook and then walks away.

You slide down the wall and sit on the floor, taking deep breaths to calm down.

AWARD YOURSELF 1 TEAMWORK POINT.

Go to the next page.

There are a lot of hard feelings swirling in your mind. You decide to try writing, like Mrs. Rogers suggested:

My name is Alec Brandon Gibbsen. I used to live with my family in Chane Valley. For now, I live with the Mediavila family, a mile away from my family's house.

Fortunately, my kid brothers—Andy, a first grader, and August, a third grader—are with me. One of the last times, though, the three of us were split up because none of the emergency homes had space for three.

This time, we were lucky. But, I guess, how lucky can we be? We're getting taken away from home because Mom and Dad are addicted to and sell prescription medication.

If that's not bad enough, social services also say the house is too messy (too unhealthy) for children. Aunt Jessy in Colorado has clean floors, clean dishes, and even open windows on beautiful days. In our home, we can't see the carpet because of clothes, garbage, and Santana's cat poop. Dirty dishes clutter every countertop. Blinds and sheets cover the windows, so no one can see what's going on inside.

You close your eyes and imagine that you're playing T-ball again. That was the beginning of your passion for baseball. You love the sport, but you also love that your dad and mom always went to your games.

One time, a girl on the team kept missing the ball as it balanced on the tee. *Swing. Miss. Swing. Miss.* She looked over at her parents and started to cry. Her mom and dad said, "You can do it!" Then your mom stood up, clapping at first, then leaning in, her hands cupped around her mouth. She shouted, "You go, girl! You can do it!" And the girl did. Your heart shot to the stars. You were so proud of the girl—and your mom.

When you started baseball, your dad taught you how to hit and your mom taught you how to throw. Your dad played baseball in high school, even went to the state championship twice (but lost both times). Your mom played softball, and her team was the area champ for three years in a row.

On your eighth birthday, your parents got out of jail and promised that things would be different. They gave you the nicest leather glove you had ever seen. For a few weeks, things really were different. Your parents took you and your brothers to play at the local diamond.

Now, those days seem like so long ago.

* * *

You sit at the Mediavilas' dining room table, trying to focus on your math homework.

Gretchen comes into the room. She's got her sweatpants on and her brown hair in a ponytail. Obviously, it's getting close to bedtime.

"Alec, someone is here to see you."

"If it's my dad, I don't want to see him."

Gretchen sighs. "He wants to say hi. I think it's nice for him to check in with you."

"He wouldn't have to be *stopping by* if he could stay out of trouble. Then we'd all be at home."

Gretchen nods. "I agree with you. But there are some things we don't understand. He needs help, and you and your brothers are like a saving grace."

You should stay at the table. That's what you want to do, and seeing your dad could make you angry enough to get into trouble. But he is still your dad, no matter what he's done. Part of you thinks you should let him say what he wants to say. What will you choose to do?

To stay at the table, go to page 22.

To talk to your dad, go to page 13.

You lie in bed, angry beyond belief. You're so mad at your parents for putting you in this position. Yet things will probably be fine in Colorado. You've always loved being with Grandma and Aunt Jessy's family.

The worst part, though, will be to leave the teammates you've played with for so long. You can't imagine your life without Puff—baseball or otherwise.

There's a soft knock at the door. Your grandma comes in and sits on your bed.

You take a deep breath. Then you say, "Moving will be hard, but it's okay. It's best for Andy and August. I have to think about them in all of this. But I'm going to miss my baseball team." That's when the tears come.

Grandma hugs you tightly. "Oh, Alec, as it turns out, your mom called. She wants you to stay. You'll be able to move back home tomorrow."

She doesn't smile. Neither do you.

AWARD YOURSELF 1 TEAMWORK POINT.

Go to page 64.

"I'm not getting a ride with you," you say. "I don't trust you."

You don't wait for him to reply. You run to Puff's car and hop into the backseat. "Can I get a ride?" you ask.

"Of course," Puff's dad answers. "I just need to make sure it's okay with your dad." He looks in your father's direction. "Okay, he's waving at me."

Puff's dad backs up the car and heads out of the park. "How was practice?" he asks.

"Awesome," Puff says. "Our first game is coming up on April 30."

Puff's dad glances at you through the rearview mirror. "Hey, Alec, you okay?" he asks.

You hoped no one would notice, but you're crying. You wish they'd keep talking to each other and not to you. You wipe your tears.

Puff's dad turns back to look at you. He starts to ask again, "Are you—"

The loudest noise you've ever heard fills your ears. *Crash!* And then you're flying . . .

And then there's pain.

For a moment—or maybe for a while—everything is cloudy in your mind. Your eyes are closed. You don't want to open them. Your heart is racing. You hear lots of sirens. You feel pebbles under the palms of your hands.

You try to focus on grabbing the pebbles and tossing them, but your head hurts so bad. So bad. Your brain isn't working right. You try to count to 100 but can't.

"Hey there, buddy," a man in a white uniform says. "What's your name?"

What *is* your name? Why does it take so long for you to remember? "Um . . . Alec."

"Okay, Alec, do you remember your birthday?" He's not looking at you as he talks. Instead, he feels all the way around your head. Then down each arm.

"December. On the seventeenth."

"Good. Do your legs hurt?"

Legs? No, they don't hurt. In fact, you can't feel your legs at all.

You might be okay eventually. Hopefully, Puff and his dad are all right, too. But one thing is certain: Your baseball season is at an end.

Go to page 75.

"Gretchen, I can't do it. Please, tell him to leave."

She nods and exits the room. A few minutes later, you hear the front door shut. Gretchen comes back in and sits down at the table.

"How are you doing?"

"I'm mad."

"I bet." She props her fist under her chin. "For what it's worth, he said to tell you he's sorry."

"Not worth a lot."

Gretchen nods. "Want to talk about what's happened at home?"

You shake your head.

"Do you need any help with your homework?"

You shake your head again.

"Good, because math and I do not get along."

You can't help but grin just a little.

"Well, I'm reading a really good mystery, so I'll be in the living room, trying to figure out whodunit." She pats your hand, then stands and leaves.

 AWARD YOURSELF 1 CONFIDENCE POINT.

Go to the next page.

You lay your head on your arms, close your eyes, and think of Florida. It's a good thing your head is down—a couple of tears escape their hiding places and land on your arm. You want to escape your life. You really do.

You sit up and look around the kitchen. You have never seen dishes spilling onto the counters or cat poop on the floor. You feel safe here.

Yes, this is probably the best place for you and your brothers. For now.

2

First Practice

Even if you can't go to Florida to watch the pros practice, it's your team's turn to start training. Last night's early-April storm dusted the fields with spring snow, but Coach Hanson let the team know you'd still be getting together.

Coach Hanson's son, Logan, is your age, and Coach has wanted to stay with Logan each year. So he's been your baseball coach pretty much since T-ball.

In the beginning, it wasn't really playing baseball. It was more just throwing and hitting. Coach introduced a few more rules at each practice and let everyone try different positions. Eventually, you landed at shortstop.

Last year, your team, the Chane Valley Cardinals, started playing in tournaments around the state. Your mom and dad sometimes showed up. A few times, they even drove you to the games. Most of the time, you rode with Coach or other parents, celebrating wins with all of them instead of your family.

Now, it's Saturday morning. First day. You're ready to put on your leather, your cleats, your cap. Gretchen's husband, Mike, will drive you to the field.

Just as you're shoveling in a forkful of scrambled eggs, Gretchen's phone rings. She answers and then looks at you, her eyes shifting to serious.

"I'll call you back." Gretchen disconnects and takes a deep breath. "Alec, that was social services. They want to have a family meeting with you, your brothers, and your parents at the jail this morning."

"I'm not going," you say.

"I know this is tough," Mike says, "but your mom wants to see you."

"Like I told Gretchen, if they didn't keep messing things up, we'd all be home right now, seeing each other all the time."

You look at your breakfast. You can't remember the last time your mom made a morning meal.

"I start spring training today," you add.

"Your first game isn't for a month," Mike says. He tries to sound casual. "I'm just saying."

You stand, your arms tight to your sides, your hands in fists. "And I'm just saying that it makes me mad!"

You look over at Andy and August, who look back at you with round eyes. You sit down again and try to slow your breathing. You pick up your fork and scoop up eggs that settle cold in your mouth.

You should visit your mom and dad, if only for your brothers. But missing the very first practice will put you behind the other players. It could cost you your starting position at shortstop. What will you choose to do?

To visit your parents, go to page 34.

To attend practice, go to page 60.

You'll meet the new kid some time, but you don't feel like talking right now. Besides, you're worried about him taking your position.

You put your equipment in your backpack and look toward the parking lot. Your dad still isn't there.

"Hey," a voice says from behind.

You turn to find the new kid. Not great.

He says, "I'm Joshua Thull. I go by J.T."

"I'm Alec Gibbsen. I go by Gibb."

You smile. He does, too.

"You're a pretty good shortstop," he tells you.

"I was thinking the same thing about you," you say.

"Well, I always wanted to be catcher, but my dad said I play a better six."

He even uses the position number to talk about baseball. He knows his stuff.

"Have you been playing long?" you ask.

"Since I was two." He shrugs. "When my mom got a new job here, my parents made sure there was a team I could play on."

Awkward silence.

You hear a honk and look at the parking lot. A man is waving right at you and your new teammate.

"That's my dad," J.T. says. He waves back. "Is your ride here?"

You scan the lot. "Nope."

"Do you want to ride with us?"

You didn't even want to talk to him, and now he's offering you a ride. Should you go with him and his dad, even if you just met him? Or is it better to wait for your parents—and hope someone actually comes? What will you choose to do?

To ride with J.T., go to page 76.

To wait for your parents, go to page 86.

You know what to do: You have to swing the bat. You've got to win this game. Fortunately, the little voice inside your head doesn't have time to taunt you again because the ball is on its way.

You love the sound of the bat smacking the baseball. You put everything you've got into your swing, and the air cracks. You watch as the ball soars into the alley between center field and left field, just like you wanted it to do.

You put your head down and take off as fast as you can. You hope the ball stays its course as you hurry toward first base.

Success! You reach the bag with ease. But . . .

Why is the other team cheering?

You look toward your bench. You see the sadness in their eyes. Your coach shakes his head, and you know the game is lost.

You turn and look to the outfield. The center fielder is on the ground, the ball in his glove. He holds it high in the air like a trophy. He caught the ball. You're out.

Just like that, the game is over.

And so is the season.

Go to the next page.

1

A New Season

You're running late, so you forget to turn your shirt right-side out. Make that a jersey: an old Saint Louis Cardinals jersey from the thrift store, to be exact. (It's #45 for Bob Gibson. You never saw the Hall of Famer play, but you have the same last name . . . sort of.)

In elementary school, you always used to wear your shirts inside out. In first grade, your teacher usually fixed it for you. By third grade, you remembered more often to get it right. In fifth grade, you only forgot once: the morning after your mom and dad got arrested.

That was the first time you went to foster care.

Now, you never get your shirt wrong. Unless you're running late because your mom got arrested again. Like last night. Your dad was taken in for questioning, too.

So in the middle of the night, you moved with your two little brothers back to foster care.

You woke up in a bed you don't know, still tired. All you want to do is move to Florida and wait for spring training to start. You could borrow someone's tent and hitchhike or take a bus as far away from Chane Valley as possible.

Yeah, right. Like that's ever going to happen.

Your foster parents, Gretchen and Mike, get all seven kids out the door and into the van. Gretchen drops you off at school just as the first bell rings.

You want to get lost in schoolwork today. You don't like science, but you love to read, especially about baseball. The library has some books on your favorite teams and players. Plus, you love to use math to figure out the players' statistics.

Unfortunately, as soon as you get to your classroom, Mrs. Rogers asks you to follow her into the hallway.

This whole school year, all seven months of it, Mrs. Rogers keeps asking if you want to talk. She's nice and all, but you don't want to tell her about your home life. It stinks. What else is there to say?

"Your shirt's inside out," she tells you politely when the two of you are alone.

You look down and feel your cheeks redden.

"Listen, Alec," she continues. "I know things can be tough at home for you and your family. Would you like to talk about it? It might make you feel better."

Your fingers reach up to your collarbone and rub—the way they always do when you feel nervous. Should you tell her what's happening? Or will you keep it to yourself? What will you choose to do?

To talk to your teacher, go to page 15.

To tell her, "No, thanks," go to page 54.

"I can't. I have homework. Just tell me what you want, so I can get back to it," you say.

"Look, I—" he begins.

"I'm so tired of you and Mom getting in trouble all the time." You try to walk past him, but he grabs your arm. His grip isn't tight.

"Alec. Son."

"Don't—"

"Please, just let me talk for a minute."

When you don't try to move away, your dad lets go of your arm.

"Being an adult is difficult. Your mom and I really struggle with some things. Just when we think things get better, we slip." He looks down and then back into your eyes. His eyes start to tear up. "I know you and your brothers expect more, but . . . some things are out of our control. We are trying so hard to get things back under control. Please, be patient with us."

The door opens. Gretchen stands there. "Everything going okay out here?" she asks.

"Yes," you say. "He was just about to leave." You walk into the house and go to your room. You're not even sure if your dad tells Gretchen good night.

Go to page 24.

You sigh. "Okay, fine, for Andy and August, I'll go." You mumble under your breath. "I just hope it doesn't cost me a spot on the team."

When you arrive at the jail, a woman named Mrs. Barry from social services meets you at the door. She takes you and your brothers to a large steel door, while Mike and Gretchen sit down and wait.

A loud bell rings, and the door opens. You follow Mrs. Barry down a hallway and into a small room with a table, chair, and couch.

"We're going to meet your parents here," Mrs. Barry says. "I'll be with you the whole time."

"How long will it take?" you ask.

"That's really up to all of you."

"I'm missing my first baseball practice."

Mrs. Barry nods at you sympathetically. She begins to answer but stops herself.

You sit on the couch and cross your arms.

A minute later, your dad walks into the room. He's wearing a clean shirt and jeans. His blond hair looks brown because it's wet, and his eyes are puffy, like he hasn't slept for days.

"Boys," your dad says excitedly, squatting down and opening his arms.

Andy and August run to him, but you stay where you are on the couch.

After hugging your brothers, your dad looks at you. "Hey, Alec, thanks for coming."

Silence.

When your mom arrives, she's escorted by a guard. Her brown hair is up in a messy ponytail. The guard moves back outside the door and shuts it. You stay on the couch. Again, your brothers run and get a hug.

She looks at you, her face beyond sad. "I understand why you're mad, but I should be out soon. Your dad and I will make different choices. I promise."

She asks about school. Then she reminds your dad to feed Santana.

You add, "And clean up his poop, too."

In a quiet but strong voice, your dad answers, "It's already cleaned. I put the litter box in the basement by the bottom of the stairs."

"What about the clothes and the papers and all the other junk?" you ask.

"Everything. I even rented a carpet cleaner, and I shampooed it all."

Wow. Maybe this is really it. Maybe this time, they'll change for good.

3

Oh, Brothers!

By the time you leave the jail, it's too late to make it to your first practice. At least Mike called Coach Hanson and explained what was going on.

You ask, "Was Coach okay with me not going?"

"He said he'd miss seeing you, but he got it."

"I suppose he knows about my family."

"Well, the good news," Mike says, "is that your dad is trying to make a new start."

You want to tell Mike the truth: that this is not the first, second, third, or even tenth time your dad has tried to make a new start. Instead, you simply say, "Yeah, I guess. It just makes me wonder how long it'll last."

For several minutes, no one speaks. But, finally, Mike says, "You and your brothers can move home soon."

You don't really want to go back, but you know that you don't have a choice.

"We're going home?" August asks from the backseat. "I don't want to."

"Oh, everything will be just fine," Mike answers.

Go to the next page.

Back at Mike and Gretchen's house, you get a call from your best friend, Wyatt Puffdon. When you two were in the third grade, you tried calling him "Dun" for a nickname. He didn't like that. A while later, you tried "Wy." Nope. That summer, "Puff" came out of your mouth. What's ironic is that he's much taller than you, and he looks like a big bad wolf couldn't blow him down. He's definitely not a "Puff." But the nickname stuck, and he's been "Puff" ever since.

"I was bummed you weren't at practice," he says. "Coach said you had a family thing. Did your parents go to jail again?"

Puff knows everything about you.

"My mom did. My dad was taken in for questioning, but he got let go. He cleaned the whole house, I guess."

"What? That's not possible," Puff jokes.

"He even cleaned the carpet with a machine."

"No way, dude. I'd have to see it to believe it."

"You may get a chance. Mike, my foster dad, said we're probably heading back home soon."

"Is that a good thing? I mean, I know your foster parents have sometimes stunk."

"Mike and Gretchen are pretty cool."

"Will you be at practice Monday night?"

"I absolutely plan on it."

After you get off the phone, you hear crying. You go downstairs and find August yelling at Andy.

"You can't play with my iPad!" shouts August.

Andy screams, "Yes, I can!"

"Hey," you say to August, "it's not your iPad. It's Mike and Gretchen's."

August glares at you. Then he throws the iPad on the couch and marches over to you. To your surprise, he punches you in the stomach.

If your parents were around, this is something they would handle. But they're not. That means you need to deal with it. Should you punish August for hitting you, like an adult would? Then again, it's been a very emotional day. Are you better off letting it go? What will you choose to do?

To punish your brother, go to page 11.

To let it go, turn to page 70.

The guy is on your team. You should introduce your-self. You go to Puff, who's putting his water bottle in his backpack.

"Let's go meet the new kid," you say.

"I did during our rapid fire drill."

"Oh, I missed that."

Puff's dad drives up.

"Gotta run," Puff says and takes off.

It looks like you're on your own. You approach your new teammate.

"Hey," you say.

He turns toward you. He nods and says, "Hi, I'm Joshua Thull. I go by J.T."

"I'm Alec Gibbsen. I go by Gibb."

You smile. He does, too.

"You're a pretty good shortstop," he tells you.

"I was thinking the same thing about you," you say.

"Well, I always wanted to be catcher, but my dad said I play a better six."

He even uses the position number to talk about base-ball. He knows his stuff.

"Have you been playing long?" you ask.

"Since I was two." He shrugs. "When my mom got a new job here, my parents made sure there was a team I could play on."

You hear a honk and look at the parking lot. A man is waving right at you and your new teammate.

"That's my dad," J.T. says. He waves back. "Is your ride here?"

You scan the lot. "Nope."

"Do you want to ride with us?"

You just met him, and now he's offering you a ride. Should you go with him and his dad? Or is it better to wait for your parents—and hope someone actually comes? What will you choose to do?

To ride with J.T., go to page 76.

To wait for your parents, go to page 86.

It's an easy choice: You have to bunt. With the third baseman hanging back, it's the perfect chance to do so.

By the time you make this decision, the baseball is already flying toward you. You grab the bat with both hands and slide it in front of you. You hold it like a shield. Your coaches always told you: Pretend like you're almost trying to catch the ball with the bat. Don't push the bat toward the ball; let the ball do all the work.

You hear a soft *thunk*, and you feel a slight shiver in your arms. The ball bounces in front of you and rolls down the third-base line. Perfect.

You take off toward first base. You run as fast as you can. You must get to first base.

Success! You reach the bag without even an attempt to throw you out. But . . .

Why is the other team cheering?

You look toward your bench. You see the sadness in their eyes. Your coach shakes his head, and you know the game is lost. You turn and look back toward home plate. Abdi is still sitting in the dirt after his slide, his head in his hands.

In that moment, you realize what a bone-headed play you made. The ball didn't have to beat you to first base. With the bases loaded, it only had to beat Abdi to home plate. By bunting the ball so short, it was an easy play for the pitcher to grab the ball and flip it to the catcher. Abdi never had a chance.

You should have smacked that baseball like your life depended on it. Instead, you lost the game. You got Abdi out at home. The season is over.

Go to page 30.

You don't say anything to your dad. You just walk over to his car. It's a 1976 Camaro that needs some work. The paint is a gritty red (except for the bumper, which is black) and the upholstery is ripping, but the engine is like brand new.

Your dad found the car online during the summer before you went to fourth grade, and you still remember that three-hour drive to buy it, how your dad was in a good place those couple of months and how you two rode with the windows down and the radio up.

You kick the tire and get into the car.

"Now, listen, Alec Brandon," your dad says after climbing in.

You don't look at him. Instead, you unzip your backpack, take out your glove, and put it on. You make a fist with your other hand and set it inside the leather.

You try to ignore him, but your dad continues. "I'm trying this time. I really am. Your mom slipped. She made a little mistake. When she gets back, things will be different."

How many times have you heard that?

"Okay," you reply. You don't know what else to say.

You listen to the sound of the engine as your dad drives through town. He keeps taking in quick breaths, like he wants to say something, but he never does.

Finally, he asks, "Want to go to Dairy Queen?"

Right this second, the last thing you want is to go anywhere with your dad. You'll be living with him again soon enough. But you should be polite. He at least deserves that.

"Thanks for the offer, but I'm tired," you say. "It was my first practice since last summer. Can you please take me back to Mike and Gretchen's?"

His shoulders slump. "Sure."

When the car pulls into the driveway, you see Mike working in the front yard. He waves at your dad.

"See ya," you say, and you start to get out.

"Alec," your dad says.

You lean back into the car.

"Alec, I . . ." He shakes his head. "See you in a couple of days."

"Okay." You hurry inside the house before he decides that he wants to talk some more.

5

Family Matters

Wednesday is here. Another practice. You can't wait. Puff's dad picks you up, and he drives to the park.

"Did you get all the answers right for that test on *The Tiger Rising*?" Puff asks.

"Yep," you reply.

"Lucky. I missed a few. Okay, a lot."

Puff's dad looks at him with a grimace.

"Sorry, Dad, but it wasn't my favorite book."

"It was an amazing book," you counter. "Can you imagine finding a tiger in your neighborhood?"

"That would be cool," he agrees.

Puff's dad drops you off at the field.

"Is your mom still getting out today?" Puff asks.

You shrug. "I didn't hear anything."

The team takes a couple of laps around the field and then stretches.

"Is winter melting out of those arms?" Coach asks.

"Yeah!" the team replies.

"Then I want to see it today."

You've heard other kids say that they don't like baseball, that it's boring, or that they don't get it. To you, it's the best sport there is: the way a baseball just rests in your hand, yearning to be thrown; the smell of the leather glove; the way it feels when you lace up your cleats, like you could run on water; the feeling in your arms when the ball connects with your bat's sweet spot and takes off like a rocket; and that split second after you dive for a ball and know that you're going to catch it. What's not to love about baseball?

Coach splits everyone into their positions. You run through drills, feeling better than you did on Monday.

For the final ten minutes, Coach again lets you choose what to work on. What will you choose to do?

To practice hitting, go to page 72.

To work on base running, go to page 73.

When practice ends, Coach calls the team over.

"Here's the schedule," he says, passing out stapled sheets. "It's got the normal rules in there, too, which you need to show your parents."

Or foster parents. Or whomever you happen to be living with at the time.

"It also has my contact information. If there's ever a question, just give me a holler. Any questions now?" He looks around at everyone, a smile on his face. "Then I'll see you on Friday."

You turn to put your stuff in your backpack, and you see your dad in his Camaro in the parking lot. In the passenger seat is your mom. It almost makes you want to barf. You don't want to deal with this right now.

"That answers my earlier question," says Puff.

"I don't know what to do. I really want to ride with you back to Mike and Gretchen's," you tell him.

"For what it's worth, I think you should ride home with them. They are your parents, after all."

You look at him. "Are you kidding? Those two who can't stay out of jail? Who can't keep their kids?"

"Yeah, I know. I was just . . ." Puff shrugs.

When your mom gets out of the car, you look at Puff. "I can't do it. I just can't."

You beeline for Puff's dad's car.

"Alec!" your mom calls. "We're here to pick you up!"

You don't respond. You get to the Puffdons' car and let yourself in.

Mr. Puffdon gets out. You sneak a look over your shoulder and see him approach your mom and dad. Your mom's arms are wrapped around her body, and you think she's crying. Your dad has his hands on his hips. You watch Mr. Puffdon's hands and head move. Whatever he says, both your mom and dad nod. He turns and heads back to the car, and your parents turn and walk toward the Camaro. You can breathe again.

"Well," Puff's dad says when he settles back into his seat, "that was tough to do. I told them you're not ready. You're just having a rough go of it right now, so they should give you some time. Sound about right?"

You look down. "Yeah, thanks."

"Let's get you back to Mike and Gretchen's."

When Puff's dad arrives at the house, he parks and then walks with you to the door. You go to your room. He stays and talks to Mike about what happened with your parents.

You stretch out on your bed, your face in the pillow. You start to cry. You're so frustrated and so sad, and all you want to do is play baseball.

The doorbell rings.

"Alec," Gretchen calls, "can you come to the door?"

Unbelievable. Did your parents follow you here?

But when you get to the front door, you see your mom's mom, Grandma Gloria.

Gretchen gets Mike, and you all sit in the living room together.

"There's no easy way to tell you this," your grandma says, "but your aunt Jessy and I are taking you and your brothers to Colorado."

"What?" you snap. "You can't!"

"Honey, I'm sorry, but we are. Your parents asked us to do this. They need some time to recoup—"

"What about my baseball team?" you ask.

She sighs. "Honey, I'm trying to do what's best—"

"What's best is that I stay with my team. If Mom and Dad need time, Mike and Gretchen can keep me, right?" Your fingers reach up to your collarbone.

"Well," Gretchen says. She sounds nervous. "We're not sure how long . . ."

You don't want to hear any more. You run back to your room and slam the door behind you.

Can this really be happening? You can't move to Colorado, away from your team. But there, at least, you won't have to deal with your parents and their problems.

Should you try to stay? If your parents need time, maybe you can live with the Puffdon family. Or will you agree to move all the way to Colorado? Perhaps that means a fresh start and some playing time on a new baseball team. What will you choose to do?

To call Puff's family, go to page 62.

To agree to move, go to page 19.

You shrug your shoulders. "Fine." You grab a glove from him and walk to the other side of the yard.

For a minute, the two of you silently toss an old baseball back and forth. The ball is hard to see with only the porch light, but you manage.

 AWARD YOURSELF 1 SKILL POINT.

"Look, I—" your dad begins.

"I'm really tired of you and Mom getting in trouble all the time."

"Alec. Son."

"Don't—"

"Please, just let me talk for a minute."

You sigh.

"Being an adult is difficult. Your mom and I really struggle with some things. Just when we think things get better, we slip." He looks down and then back into your eyes. His voice cracks. "I know you and your brothers expect more, but . . . some things are out of our control. We are trying so hard to get things back under control. Please, be patient with us."

The door opens. Gretchen stands there.

"Everything going okay out here?" she asks.

"Yes," you say. "He was just about to leave."

You hand your dad the old glove and walk into the house. You're not even sure if your dad tells Gretchen good night.

Go to page 24.

"I'm fine," you say. But you can't help it; you start to cry.

Mrs. Rogers pats your back. Sobs form in your belly and then bark from your mouth.

"If you want, I can give you this notebook," says Mrs. Rogers. She holds it up to show you; it looks new. "You can write how you're feeling, and I can write back."

You remain silent, except for the sobs.

She smiles. "I do have to be honest. If you write about something unsafe, I'll have to show the social worker. We want you to be safe in your foster family."

You nod.

"Okay, good. Stay out here as long as you need to." She hands you the notebook and then walks away.

You slide down the wall and sit on the floor, taking deep breaths to calm down.

Go to page 16.

You sit on the couch. "Andy, pause that game and come here."

He snuggles close to you and puts his thumb in his mouth. You gently guide his thumb back to his lap.

"Try not to do that. Remember?" you say.

Andy sits on his hands.

"You're young, but you've been through more than most kids. So I'm going to be honest with you. I want to love Mom and Dad. But I just don't, not right now."

Andy's eyes grow wide. "You don't?"

You take a deep breath. "I take that back. I love them, but I don't like them. They're making stupid choices."

"Don't say *stupid*."

"Sorry, they're making bad choices. They've got you, me, and August, but they're not being good parents."

Andy nuzzles himself even closer to your body. He's a great kid. He deserves some hope. So you add, "But Dad did clean the house . . ."

AWARD YOURSELF 1 CONFIDENCE POINT.

Go to the next page.

4

Practice Time

Finally. Second practice. And you're here this time. It's a warm day. The snow is already gone. You've got your glove snug on your hand. You've got your cleats on your feet. You've got your cap square on your head.

"Let's stretch it out a little, boys," Coach Hanson yells. "We still have winter frozen in our bodies."

Coach has you all jog around the diamond a couple of times. Then you and the other 14 players circle your arms, stretch your wrists, and move your elbows behind your backs and in front of your chests.

It feels so good to be out here again. Your body and mind have been waiting to get onto the field.

Next, you practice your throwing drills.

"Loosen up, boys," says Coach.

He tells you to step to the side to throw and catch, and then he has you run backward, then catch fly balls. You smile. Not only is this easy for you, it's fun.

For the next 20 minutes, you work on drills at your position on the field, while pitchers and catchers go to another part of the field with an assistant coach. You work on all sorts of throws with Puff and the rest of the infield players: wrist flips, rockers, and long and short levers. You have to admit that you feel a little rust—or what Coach calls "winter"—in your arms and legs, but you know that it'll go away quickly with each practice.

For the final ten minutes, the coaches let you choose what to work on. You can practice base running and sliding, or you can work on hitting. What will you choose to do?

To practice hitting, go to page 68.

To work on base running, go to page 69.

"Boys," Coach Hanson yells, "fall in." He waits for everyone to gather. "I'll get the game schedule to you Wednesday. Practices are Mondays, Wednesdays, and Fridays unless we have games. You have the talent to play the best teams in the state. I'm proud of you all."

You notice your dad standing by the fence. What is he doing here?

"—to think about for Wednesday's practice." Coach looks around at all the boys. "Questions?"

"When's our first game, Coach?" Puff asks.

"April 30. Think we'll be ready?"

"Yeah," the boys answer.

"It doesn't sound like it to me. Do you think you'll be ready?"

"*Yeah!*" The boys shout this time.

Coach says, "Head on home."

You look at your dad again, and you wonder where home is. After grabbing your things and shoving them into your backpack, you walk over to him.

"Hey, Alec. Ready to go?" he says.

"Mike's picking me up."

"No, I texted him. I told him I'd do it."

You can't help it. You speak before you think. "How about you let me decide who I want to pick me up? I want Mike. Mike said he could."

58

Your dad's smile disappears. "I told Mike I'd do it. He's busy with all the other kids. I'm helping him out."

"Gee, thanks."

"That's enough of the attitude, Alec. I'm trying. Just appreciate that, okay? I'm taking you to his house today, but your mom should be out of jail in a couple of days. Then we get you kids back."

You see Puff waiting by his car. You can ride home with him if you want. Should you hop in with your friend and his family, or can you trust your dad enough to drive you? What will you choose to do?

To ride with Puff, go to page 20.

To ride with your dad, go to page 44.

"Forget it," you say. "I won't see them."

"I have to disagree with you, Alec," Gretchen says.

"No offense, but you don't know what it's like to have parents in jail."

Gretchen nods. "Touché."

You turn and say to Mike, "Can you please drive me to practice?"

* * *

Your team warms up in the chilly April morning, and you know that this is where you need to be: with your friends, not your parents.

After stretches and drills, the coach says he wants to practice hitting, just to work out the kinks.

You're on deck, so you practice swinging. Your arms feel good, your shoulders feel strong, and your hands grip the bat as if they didn't let go all winter.

You're up.

You miss the first two pitches. On the third one, you slap a soaring fly ball into the gap between left and center field. You start to run toward first base, but your feet aren't as ready as your upper body. They tangle together and you fall, your right wrist slamming into the frozen ground.

The next thing you know, you're on your way to the hospital. Your wrist is swollen, and it throbs with pain.

Not long after that, an x-ray shows broken bones in five places.

The doctor says, "This is a very severe injury. You'll need to have surgery—and you'll probably never play baseball again."

Go to page 75.

This is not how things are supposed to happen. Kids are supposed to stay with their parents. The parents are not supposed to break the law.

You decide to call Puff. Maybe his parents can help you. You dial the number to his house. Puff answers on the second ring.

"Hey, what's up?" he asks.

"I need your parents' help."

Puff seems to understand at once. "Mom? Dad?" he calls. "Can you come here?"

You wait as Puff talks to his parents for a moment. You feel good about your decision. You hear the click of another phone being activated.

"Hey, Alec," Puff's dad says.

There's another click.

"Hi, Alec," Puff's mom chimes in.

"What's up?" Mr. Puffdon asks.

"I kind of need your family's help," you begin. "You know my parents keep messing up, and now it sounds like Mike and Gretchen can't keep me much longer for some reason. Mom just got out of jail, but I'm afraid . . ." You swallow hard. "I just need a place to stay for the rest of the baseball season. Then I'll probably move out to Colorado."

Then there's silence for several long seconds.

At last, Mr. Puffdon says, "This is something we need to discuss, Alec. You're a great kid, but we have to figure this out as a family and talk to yours about it first."

"Okay, I get it," you say, suddenly feeling deflated. You rub your collarbone and silently beg yourself not to start crying.

"Look, Alec," Mrs. Puffdon says, "I know that's not what you wanted to hear. But what you're asking for is a big responsibility."

"So, right now," Puff's dad says, "the best we can do is get the conversation going."

"Thank you," you say, quickly swiping the tears from your face.

"Are Mike and Gretchen able to talk for a minute?" asks Mr. Puffdon.

"Let me check," you reply.

You put Mike and Gretchen on the phone with Puff's dad, and he tells them about your idea.

"Well, as it turns out," Gretchen says, "his mom called here. The boys will be able to move back into their house tomorrow."

She doesn't smile. Neither do you.

6

Going Home

After school, you and your brothers ride on your old bus again. You're moving back in with you parents.

When you get home, it's just like your dad said it would be: practically spotless. You can see the carpet. All the trash is gone. The sheets are off the windows. Santana sits on top of the couch (with just its cushions rather than piles of clothes). Her tail flicks, and she looks at you with her bright blue eyes.

You throw your backpack on the floor near the door and jump onto the couch. "Hey, Santana Siamese," you say, stroking her brown ears and head, then her beige back, then down to her chocolate-brown tail.

"Boys," your mom calls from the kitchen, "I made you a snack."

Again, you're surprised—the kitchen is spotless. No more dishes in the sink, no papers or mail cluttering the counters, no Santana poop on the floor. Instead, you find slices of apple, cheese, and crackers, even a glass of milk on the small wooden table.

You and your brothers sit down, and your mom takes a chair, too. "How was school today?" she asks.

"We learned about sink and float," Andy says.

Mom asks, "What sinks?"

"Metal."

"What floats?"

"A feather."

She smiles at him and then turns. "August?"

"We went to the Tonka Nature Center and saw some turtles because they're done hibernating."

"Your dad and I have taken you boys there a few times." She smiles and then looks at you. "Alec?"

You aren't sure which part to tell her. You certainly don't want to tell her everything. You aren't ready to have serious conversations, yet.

"A plot line for stories," you finally say. "The line goes up for the introduction and rising action. Then there's the climax, or most emotional part. Then it goes down to the conclusion."

"Every story has its ups and downs," she adds.

You look her in the eyes. "Yep," and you try to send her a brain message: *more up, less down, Mom.* Then you ask, "What time is it? I have practice soon."

"Oh, right, I'll take you. Dad won't be home."

When your mom drops you off at the field, it's like you were let out of a cage. This is where you relax, where you take deep breaths, where you don't have to worry about your mom and dad messing up.

You throw the ball around with Puff until the coach calls the team over.

"Boys, I've got some news. This guy," he nods to a kid you've never seen before. "He's new to Chane Valley. He and his family moved here from Saint Paul."

The new kid is almost as tall as Puff but not as big. He smiles. You want to be nice to him. After all, if things don't work out with your parents, you could become the new kid in some other town.

Coach finishes, "His name is Joshua Thull. He plays the shortstop position."

Crud.

"Let's get practicing."

You start to run off with the rest of the team, but Coach says, "Gibb, come here."

You turn back.

"Let's see how this plays out. No worries about losing your position."

"Okay." What else are you supposed to say?

"Go join the infield. Show me what you got."

You run out to start drills, but your head is heavy with thoughts of the new player. Despite what Coach said, you're worried. How good is he?

Fifteen minutes later, you have an answer to your own question: He's good, all right. He's got the hands, and he's got the feet. Now you're *really* worried.

At the end of practice, you don't see your dad anywhere in the parking lot. Joshua is putting his things in his backpack. Now would be a good time to introduce yourself. You never did during practice; the coaches kept you moving. But, then again, what if he ends up taking your position? Do you really want to be friendly to him when you'll be battling for playing time on the field? What will you choose to do?

To introduce yourself, go to page 40.

To leave, go to page 27.

AWARD YOURSELF 2 SKILL POINTS.

Go to page 58.

Go to page 58.

"Ow, that hurt!" you snap. "Not cool, August. You need to chill out." You put your arms over your belly. "And you're going to tell me you're sorry."

"No way! I hate you! I hate everybody!"

August runs to his room just as Gretchen makes it downstairs. "What's going on?" she asks.

You explain what happened. You also tell her what August said in the car. Gretchen thanks you and leaves to find your brother.

Andy is no longer crying, but he's sitting on the floor. His chest rises in short bursts of breath.

"August is mean," Andy hisses.

"Did you take the iPad from him?"

"No, he took it from me."

"Okay, it's over." You pick the iPad off the couch and hand it to him.

Andy goes back to the game he was playing, still trying to catch his breath.

"Alec," Andy says without looking away from the screen, "when do we see Mom and Dad again?"

"I don't know."

"Do you love them?"

Good question.

"Because I love them," Andy adds.

You hope that's the end of it because you really don't know what to say, but Andy looks at you impatiently.

"Well, do you?"

There's no simple answer. You know that you should love your parents, but the truth is you don't even like them right now. Andy probably isn't old enough to understand that. Should you be honest with him, even if it might confuse him or hurt his feelings? Or is lying to him the better option? What will you choose to do?

To tell the truth, go to page 55.

To lie to your brother, go to page 14.

AWARD YOURSELF 2 SKILL POINTS.

If this is the *same* choice as last time, also . . .

 AWARD YOURSELF 2 MORE SKILL POINTS.

Go to page 48.

AWARD YOURSELF 2 SPEED POINTS.

If this is the *same* choice as last time, also . . .

AWARD YOURSELF 2 MORE SPEED POINTS.

Go to page 48.

You step out of the box again to practice your swing. You don't mean for it to happen—and you sure don't want it to—but thoughts of your parents sneak into your mind. These are the parents of long ago, the ones who spent time with you at the baseball field, who cheered you on as you learned the sport. These are your parents who starred in softball and baseball. These are your parents who are *not* users or sellers . . . or criminals.

You shake away the thoughts and step back in.

The pitcher winds up . . .

Your parents are *users.*

The ball hurtles toward you . . .

Your parents are *sellers.*

You swing with all of your might . . .

Your parents are *criminals.*

Strike three.

You're out before you even have the chance to run the bases and make it home. The bat drops from your hands, and you close your eyes. You hear the Storm cheer, and you feel sick. You can't believe it; you lost the final game for your team, again.

Go to the next page.

GAME
OVER

Try again.

To be honest, you still don't trust your parents. If you don't leave now, you might be here all night. Of course, you know better than to ride with a stranger without letting your parents know.

"Sure, I'll catch a ride," you say. "But does your dad have a cell phone? I need to call my dad."

J.T. chuckles. "I have a cell phone. You don't?"

You feel your cheeks turn red. "My mom and dad don't have the money for me to get one."

"Oh, yeah, that's cool." J.T. digs in his backpack and pulls out his phone.

You dial your dad's number. He doesn't answer, so you call your mom. You tell her how you're getting home, and she promises to let your dad know, too.

When J.T. introduces you to his father, his dad says, "Nice to meet you. Where are we headed?"

"I live on Mitchell Drive. Oh, wait, no, I don't. I just moved back with my parents," you blurt.

Oops.

J.T. glances at you over his shoulder, and you see Mr. Thull look at you in the rearview mirror.

"Sorry, long story. I live on Jefferson Avenue now," you tell them.

"I hope you know where that is," Mr. Thull says. "I still don't know Chane Valley very well."

"Sure. Just keep going straight over the bridge."

The car stops at a red light in front of a gas station. You notice your dad's Camaro in the parking lot. He's talking to—or arguing with—another man.

Your dad is standing tall, and his hands are balled into fists. He's definitely not smiling. The other guy is also standing tall, his back wide under a muscle shirt.

You immediately wonder if it's a drug deal gone bad. But your dad promised that things are different now. You wonder if you should have Mr. Thull drop you off.

If your dad is about to get into a fight, maybe you can stop it. You do not want him to go to jail again. On the other hand, you might walk into a dangerous situation. What will you choose to do?

To stop now, go to page 95.

To say nothing, go to page 114.

You signal for a time out. Then you run to the bench. "Coach," you say. You look past him at her. "My mom."

Coach Hanson looks over his shoulder. Your mom is now lying on the hood.

"Go," he says.

You run past the bleachers and signal to your dad to follow you. Then you race to the car. The closer you get to her, the more you hear her sobs.

"Mom, are you okay? What's wrong?"

She moves her arm away from her eyes. Her nose is red, her eyes are red, and her hair is a tangle.

Your dad nudges you to the side and helps her to sit up. Then he helps her ease into the car.

"Go finish your game, Alec. I'll sit with her."

"Is she okay?"

"Yeah. Just . . . bummed." He sighs. "To be honest, I don't work much, and she just got laid off."

"She got fired?"

"Her company didn't need her anymore. But it's not because she did anything wrong."

"If you guys aren't working, what does that mean for us—for our family?"

"We don't know, yet. We have to decide what to do. But don't worry; we'll work it out. Now, go on. This is an important game."

"But—"

"Focus on the game. Support your team."

You nod, although you don't believe him, and then you run back to the field.

"Sorry, Coach," you say.

"I get it, Gibb. It's okay."

You sit on the bench and watch. You're down, 3–1. J.T. is at shortstop.

Maybe you bring good luck, though. Abdi catches a fly ball, and the half-inning ends.

In the Cardinals' next turn at bat, Ashton hits a line drive into the gap and makes it to third. You'd be up next, but instead it's J.T. You admire his stance, the way he holds the bat like he was born with it.

When the bat connects with the ball, the tiny white orb arcs up, up, up . . . . It doesn't land until it passes over the fence in center field.

"Well, I'll be!" Coach exclaims.

It's a home run. You and the rest of the guys jump up and meet J.T. at home plate. The score is tied, 3–3.

The game progresses in a flurry of hits and runs. Both teams seem to score at will. The Silver manage nine runs throughout the game. But Puff's eighth-inning double— with the bases loaded—gives the Cardinals their ninth, tenth, and eleventh runs.

Your team leaves as the winner, 11–9. That means you advance to the state championship!

When you get back to the family car, your mom is no longer crying. She grins at you, gets out, and hugs you. "Congratulations."

You climb into the backseat with a grin of your own. Part of you wants to be upset that you came out of the game, but you're too happy about the team's big win.

After your brothers are in bed, your parents knock at your bedroom door. When they come in, your dad says, "Mom and I need to go out and chat for a bit. Can you handle things here?"

"Sure," you say, although you get a knot in your stomach. Where are they going? Why now?

Both of them come and kiss you on the forehead. "See you in the morning," your mom says.

Go to the next page.

Smash! Clang!

You open your eyes. The bedroom is dark. You roll over and look at your clock. It's 2:31 a.m.

You register another sound: your parents yelling.

Not again.

You hear words like *money, work, mortgage, family,* and *blame.*

They sound extremely mad. This argument could get ugly. Should you stay in your room and keep out of it? Or is it better to go out there and try to calm them down? What will you choose to do?

To stay in your room, go to page 145.

To go out and talk to them, go to page 122.

You touch your collarbone, and you close your eyes. You're part of this team. You're helping your teammates by playing in right field.

You bring your hand down. You open your eyes and look over your shoulder at Gretchen and Mike. Mike catches your eye and waves. You smile and nod.

Game on.

 AWARD YOURSELF 1 TEAMWORK POINT.

Go to the next page.

The Cardinals go down quietly in the bottom of the sixth, so you return to right field. The inning begins with two easy outs. The third batter pops up between J.T. and Ashton.

J.T. calls for it. The ball thumps into his glove . . . and then rolls out, onto the ground. It's his second error of the game.

He grabs the ball and tries to recover, but it's too late. The runner is halfway to second base, and no one on your team is even close to the bag. J.T. can only hold the ball as the player glides to the open base.

"Come on now, boys," Coach says. "No runs."

The next batter drives the ball past Puff. The runner on second makes it home before you can throw the ball back to the infield.

Tie game.

In the bottom of the inning, the Cardinals go down, 1-2-3. Coach doesn't say a word, just grips the fence.

In the top of the eighth, the Storm manage to load the bases in between two outs.

No taters, no taters, no taters. Four runs would be bad.

You glance into the stands. Gretchen's hands cover her face, but her fingers are spread enough to see. Mike clasps his hands in front of him. August watches you intently. Andy watches a plane in the sky.

No matter what happens today, I just want to go home with the Mediavilas. You know that you shouldn't be thinking about it right now, but you can't help it.

When the batter swings, the bat *cracks.* The hit heads toward J.T. He bobbles it in the dirt but quickly digs it out and throws to first.

"Safe!" the umpire calls.

Everyone advances one base, including the runner who was at third. Now the Storm lead, 4–3.

The next batter hits a long fly that causes you to swallow your breath for a second. But Julian runs under it and makes the catch for out number three.

Your team answers in the bottom of the eighth by loading the bases, but three outs come before any runs do. You head into the final inning, behind by one run.

Go to the next page.

You grab your glove and start for right field when you hear Coach call, "Gibb!"

You turn and see Coach Hanson standing beside J.T., who has his head down. He kicks at the dirt.

"J.T. seems a bit rattled out there," Coach says. "He's committed a few errors, so he wants to know if you'd like your old position back."

How many teamwork points do you have?

If you have three points or more, go to page 89.

If you have two or fewer points, go to page 110.

"I think I'd better wait for my parents," you say.

"No problem," replies J.T. "It was nice to meet you. I'll see you at school."

He jogs to his dad's car. You watch as they drive away. Then you look back toward the field. The coaches are gone. They must have assumed you left, so they did the same. You're all alone.

AWARD YOURSELF 1 CONFIDENCE POINT.

You wait . . .

. . . and wait . . .

. . . and wait.

You wish you knew what time it is. The sky isn't dark yet, but it will be soon enough.

A familiar car approaches, and you wave vigorously. It isn't your family's car, though. It's J.T. and his dad.

They pull up next to you, and J.T. rolls down the window. "You're still here? Good thing we drove past. Have you changed your mind about that ride?" he asks.

"Yes, I'll take a ride," you say. "But does your dad have a cell phone? I need to call my dad."

J.T. chuckles. "I have a cell phone. You don't?"

You feel your cheeks turn red. "My mom and dad don't have the money for me to get one."

"Oh, yeah, that's cool." J.T. digs in his backpack and pulls out his phone.

You dial your dad's number. He doesn't answer, so you call your mom. This is not the time to start a fight, so you just tell her how you're getting home. She promises to let your dad know, too.

When J.T. introduces you to his father, Mr. Thull says, "Nice to meet you. Where are we headed?"

"I live on Mitchell Drive. Oh, wait, no, I don't. I just moved back with my parents," you blurt.

Oops.

J.T. glances at you over his shoulder, and you see Mr. Thull look at you in the rearview mirror.

"Sorry, long story. I live on Jefferson Avenue now," you tell them.

"I hope you know where that is," Mr. Thull says. "I still don't know Chane Valley very well."

"Sure. Just keep going straight over the bridge."

The car stops at a red light in front of a gas station. You notice your dad's Camaro in the parking lot. He's talking to—or arguing with—another man. Your dad is standing tall, and his hands are balled into fists. He's definitely not smiling.

The other guy is standing tall, too, his back wide under a muscle shirt.

You immediately wonder if it's a drug deal gone bad. But your dad promised that things are different now. You wonder if you should have Mr. Thull drop you off.

If your dad is about to get into a fight, maybe you can stop it. You do not want him to go to jail again. On the other hand, you might walk into a dangerous situation. What will you choose to do?

To stop now, go to page 95.

To say nothing, go to page 114.

You smile and slap J.T. on the back. "No way! This guy's a great shortstop. I know he can do it, Coach. Let him finish the game."

J.T.'s head snaps up. He gapes at you, mouth open.

You look him straight in the eyes. "Did you hear me? Let's get out there and win this."

A confident smile stretches across his face. He nods and says, "Let's do it."

You run to your position in right field and settle into your stance. You're the team's right fielder. You're going to help the Cardinals win.

Your excitement dwindles, though, as Logan walks the first batter. The second batter singles on a soft grounder to third. That puts runners on first and second with nobody out. Your team is already down by a run; you can't afford to let them score again.

Logan bounces back nicely. He strikes out the next batter. That means a double play will end the inning. You find yourself hoping for a ground ball to J.T. He could stop the Storm's turn at bat with just one play.

Your wish is granted . . . sort of. The batter screams a ground ball toward the gap between J.T. and Landon. It's an impossible play, one that you know *you* couldn't make. When the ball passes between your teammates, the lead runner will score from second with ease . . .

Except the ball never passes between your team-mates. You see J.T. leave his feet. He dives toward the baseball. He stretches his glove as far as he can. If you didn't know better, you'd say his arm grew six inches. The baseball slides into the pocket of his glove.

J.T. doesn't have time to stand, turn, and throw. There's no way he'll beat the runner to first base. But Landon, right next to him, is already standing and already facing Puff.

J.T. flips the baseball to Landon. Landon snags it with his right hand and fires a dart that hits Puff's glove with a *snap*.

"Out!" yells the umpire at first.

Your jaw drops open. Your eyes bulge. That might have been the greatest play you've ever seen.

The runners who were at first and second are now on second and third. But at least there are two outs. You're one play away from getting out of this inning. Of course, the Storm are one play away from putting this game out of reach. A base hit to the outfield will put you behind by three runs.

Logan's arm is tired. You can tell by how wild his pitches are getting. Four balls in a row put yet another player on base. So, with the bases loaded, Zachary Tyler steps up to the plate.

Coach Hanson calls, "Timeout," and walks to the mound. He gathers the infielders together. They could be talking about anything: baseball, the movies, which restaurant has the best hamburgers. This is just to give Logan a minute to rest.

When play resumes, it looks as if that short break did the trick. Zachary swings and misses. Then he swings and misses again. But on his third swing, he connects.

The ball seems to leap off his bat. It zooms into the air, heading toward the gap between you and Julian. You might be able to get to it, but you'll have to run faster than you've ever run before.

Add together your speed points and your talent points. How many points do you have?

If you have three or more points, go to page 127.

If you have two or fewer points, go to page 138.

"Yeah, Coach," you say, "good idea. Getting him some game-time experience will be good for the team."

Part of you is nervous that you just handed J.T. your position for the rest of the season. But, deep down, you know that you have the talent and the skill to keep your spot at shortstop.

"You've played a good game," adds Coach. "I don't want you out of the lineup. Go and take over for Abdi in right field."

You hurry to the outfield, keeping an eye on J.T. He looks like he *belongs* at shortstop.

He doesn't make a mistake. Not once. Your team holds the visitors to their one run.

At bat, J.T. walks with two outs, but he's stranded there; the third out comes on the very next pitch.

Coach stands in front of the bench, studying his lineup card. "Gibb," he says, "move back to shortstop. I want to try J.T. at catcher."

Thrilled, you jog to your position.

The first batter hits a line drive to Puff. Easy out. The second batter flies out to Julian. The third batter smacks a towering pop up. It glides right to you. Another easy out . . . until the ball slips through your glove and *thuds* onto the ground.

You don't believe it: runner on first.

Embarrassed beyond belief, you pick up the ball and throw it to Logan. Then you smack the leather a few times with your fist. You put your head low and look under your brim at your family. They're still there.

The next batter hits a ground ball to you.

Instead of hitting your glove, the baseball passes through your legs, and you scramble to grab it. You manage to clutch it, but when you throw to Puff, your aim is off. The ball soars over his head.

A runner crosses home plate before Puff gets control of the baseball and throws it to Landon on third.

"Shake it off," Ashton tells you.

Okay, yes, shake it off.

"Let's go, Cardinals!" Julian yells.

When another ground ball bounces toward you, you imagine yourself messing up again—and you do. You grab it, drop it, and then fumble to find it.

At least this time, you prevent the lead runner from scoring. But now he's on third. Crud.

Fortunately, the next hit flies straight to Gabriel in left field. He catches it, putting you out of your misery.

When you run into the dugout, you expect the coach to pull you aside and bench you. He doesn't.

You grab a bat and warm up your swing, hoping that you don't mess up again.

But you do. Three strikes, you're out.

You sit on the bench, wishing you could make yourself disappear. This would be a good time for J.T. to replace you again. Should you ask Coach to put him back in at shortstop? You're less likely to make a mistake in right field. Or will you try shortstop again? What will you choose to do?

To move to right field, go to page 109.

To stay at shortstop, go to page 116.

"Mr. Thull, I'm sorry," you quickly say, "but can you stop at that gas station? I see my dad." Your fingers go straight for your collarbone.

Mr. Thull puts on the brakes and turns the car into the parking lot.

"He's over there," you say, "by the trash cans."

"He looks a bit mad right now," Mr. Thull notes, but he pulls up next to the two men. He puts the car in park and gets out.

"Sorry to interrupt, gentlemen, but I believe I have Mr. Gibbsen's son with me."

Your dad looks surprised. He turns to you as you climb out the back door. "Now isn't a good time, Alec," he says.

"You forgot me at the baseball field."

He closes his eyes for a moment. He opens them and looks at the man across from him. "We'll talk later."

The man leans in close to your dad and whispers something. Then he walks away.

Mr. Thull steps toward your dad and sticks out his hand. "I'm Ira Thull. My son is J.T. We just moved here. The boys are on the same baseball team."

Your dad takes a deep breath and shakes Mr. Thull's hand. "I'm Brandon, Alec's dad. I suppose you offered him a ride when I didn't show up?"

"Yep. No problem. Alec called his mom first."

"Good." Your dad looks at you. "Let's head home, buddy. Thanks for offering him a ride, Ira."

"My pleasure. See you later, Alec."

"Yeah, thanks."

When you get in the Camaro, you have to ask: "Who was that guy? Why did you look so mad?"

Dad hesitates. "A former friend, let's say. He's mad at me." He pauses, as if trying to choose the right words. Eventually, he finishes. "Let's leave it at that, okay?"

"Sure."

The rest of the ride home is quiet. You can't help but wonder what would have happened if you didn't ask Mr. Thull to stop. Well, at least, part of you wonders. The other part just wants to pretend it never happened, that your dad came and picked you up in the first place. For as many times as you've been told to "leave it at that" over the years, you worry that you can't. Your fingers find your collarbone yet again.

7

The First Game

April 30. *Finally.* You didn't think the first game would ever get here. You've practiced and worked hard, and you feel more than ready. J.T. has been practicing at both shortstop and catcher, and you two have even been hanging out at school.

The first game is a home game. (And speaking of home, things at your house are still going well, too.)

You see your parents in the bleachers. They brought your brothers. Mike and Gretchen brought their foster kids to the game, too. You can't help but smile. Your whole family is here.

The team you're playing is from a couple of hours away. Two years ago, you blew them out, winning by nine runs. Last year, it was another win but only by a run. If they improved again, today will be interesting.

In the team huddle, you stand next to Puff and J.T.

"Okay, boys," Coach says, "this is a good team. We need to play hard. Ready, 1-2-3, Cardinals!"

You run to your position and settle in, between Ashton at second base and Landon at third. You feel your adrenaline pumping. This is what you wait for, through fall and winter. Your glove is tight on your hand. You smack your fist into it, bend your knees, and lean forward. You're ready.

Logan's first pitch is a strike: a great way to start. The next pitch is another strike. You don't even twitch. Your coach says that you must always look cool until the end of the game. Celebrate runs, yes—but don't celebrate each and every good moment. Concentrate. Get through each pitch, each out, each inning.

Logan's first out is a strikeout. Awesome.

The next batter hits the ball right to you, practically a can of corn that rises high into the air and then lands directly in your glove. Two outs.

The third batter, however, smashes a hit into the gap between Julian in center field and Abdi in right field. Julian throws to Ashton at second, forcing the batter to stay at first base with Puff.

After that, a hit soars over Gabriel's head in left field. The runner at first speeds his way around the bases—all the way to home plate, scoring a run. The batter gets stopped at second. It's a good thing he wasn't as fast.

Logan strikes out the next batter for the third and final out of the half-inning.

Your team jogs to the dugout. It's Chane Valley's turn to bat. The top of the order gets ready. Ben, the leadoff, is the best hitter the Cardinals have. He takes the first pitch for a strike. The second pitch connects square on the sweet spot of Ben's swing. Home run! Ben rounds the bases, and, just like that, it's a tie game, 1–1.

You take a quick look at the bleachers. Your family and the Mediavilas are still there. It's not really like you expected them to be gone. You just want to make sure that you're not dreaming.

Up next, Gabriel hits a line drive to third and hustles to first base. Safe.

Ashton repeats the hit with another shot toward third base. He, too, is safe. Gabriel advances to second.

Now it's your turn to hit. You're ready. You're not even nervous.

You watch two strikes and one ball go by before you take your first swing. That fourth pitch looks hittable on its way. Your bat connects, and you feel a *twang*.

It's a Baltimore chop, hitting the ground and then bouncing over the pitcher's head. You run as fast as you can to the bag. The second baseman doesn't grab the ball cleanly, so everyone is safe.

Now the bases are loaded, and it's Puff's turn to hit. He's one of the strongest batters, the meat of the order. Puff practices his swing and then steps into the batter's box. The pitcher seems to find his stuff because Puff strikes out on three pitches. One out.

Logan is next, and he likes the first pitch he sees. He hits a triple, clearing the bases. You sprint to home plate, giving your team a 4–1 lead.

The inning ends after Julian and Abdi strike out.

Go to the next page.

The next three innings go by in a blur of strikeouts and ground balls. Neither team gets on the board.

Just as you're about to run onto the field for inning number five, Coach calls you over.

"Gibb, I'm thinking about trying J.T. at shortstop. I want to see how he performs in a game. What do you think? It's your call. I'll leave it up to you."

Add up your talent points and your skill points. How many points do you have?

If you have four or more points, go to page 92.

If you have three or fewer points, go to page 136.

You've played shortstop since you first started baseball, and now your coach is taking it away from you. You pack up your stuff and wait for Puff. His dad is taking you back to your foster home.

"I'm so excited for tomorrow's game!" Puff exclaims.

You don't say anything.

"Aren't you?" he asks.

"Coach moved me to right field, and J.T. gets to play my position."

"Oh, man, that's a bummer." He turns and cups his hands to his mouth. "J.T., Ashton, Landon, Logan!" The players are still tossing the ball around. "Come here!"

Your teammates jog over to you.

"What's up?" Logan asks.

Puff looks at you. "Tell 'em."

"Coach moved me to right field," you say. "J.T.'s in at shortstop."

"Oh, probably because Abdi sprained his ankle," Landon notes.

"But then I should be in right field," J.T. replies.

"Why?" you ask. "You're better at shortstop."

"I like playing all the positions, Alec. I'm utility. No big deal. I'll talk to Coach."

"No, you stay at shortstop. I guess Coach knows what he's doing. I'll move to right field."

Puff's dad drives you to the Jacksons'.

As soon as you walk in the door, Mrs. Jackson has news. "Your mom and dad want you to visit them in jail," she says.

"No way," you reply. "We tried that before, and it was terrible." Your fingers find your collarbone. If you rub hard enough, you wonder if a genie will pop out of thin air and grant you three wishes. Wish one: never visit your parents in jail again.

"You don't have a choice," Mrs. Jackson answers.

"I did last time."

"Now you don't. You'll go and see them. Period. End of discussion." She walks out of the room, and you hear her car keys jangle. "Andy! August! Get in the car."

Mrs. Barry from social services is waiting at the jail again. She leads you and your brothers down the hallway but stops before you reach the room.

"It's going to be hard to see your mom and dad, but they felt it was important. They want to stay positive, and they need your support. To help them, please try and be brave. Try not to cry or be angry with them. Do you think you can do that?"

Andy looks up at you. So does August.

You nod.

Mrs. Barry leads you into the room, and you sit on the couch between your brothers. Andy scoots closer to you and lays his head on your arm.

Your dad arrives first. His hair is messy, his eyes are puffy, and he looks weak—like he hasn't eaten in days. You wonder if it's because he hasn't been able to take any drugs or if he's worried about you and your brothers.

Andy jumps up to hug your dad. You and August both cross your arms and remain seated.

"Boys," your dad begins, but he looks down and stops. He turns around, combs his hair with his hand, and then turns back. He takes a deep breath. "Thanks for coming." He focuses on you. "Alec, your game, I hope it goes well."

"Thanks."

"Cheer him on for me, okay, August and Andy?"

The door opens, and your mom comes in. Her long hair is gone. Now, it barely falls to where her earrings should be. You hate it.

"Hi, boys," she whispers, and Andy runs to hug her.

You and August still don't get up. Your mom starts to cry as she keeps hugging your little brother.

When Andy lets go of her, he says, "Mommy, we need to be brave. No more crying."

You can't tell if she laughs or cries.

11

The Championship

Saturday finally arrives, and with it comes the state championship game. Your opponent is the Nevisville Storm, a team you guys have never played before.

"They're a good team from up north," says Coach Hanson. "Their best player is at second base: Zachary Tyler. But you're a good team, too, with a whole bunch of great players. So let's go get 'em!"

Your team gathers around. You each put a fist in the middle of the circle. "Ready, 1-2-3, Cardinals!

You run to the outfield, telling yourself that everything will be fine. You think of J.T. and how he's a good utility player. You force yourself to think that way, too.

You turn toward the diamond and take your stance. Then you scan the stands. You see almost all the players' families. But no Gretchen or Mike. You thought that they might come.

Logan strikes out the Storm's first two batters. The Tyler kid hits a single, but Logan gets batter number four to ground out.

It's time for the Cardinals to get on base.

Ben pops out to Tyler. One out. Gabriel chops the ball to third base and beats the throw to first. Ashton grounds out to first, but Gabriel is able to move over to second. Two outs.

You take a few practice swings, and then you step to the plate. You like the first pitch you see. It seems as big as a bowling ball. You swing, and . . .

Smack!

The baseball shoots into center field and bounces in front of their outfielder. He scoops it up but bobbles it. You don't hesitate. You slide in at second base, just ahead of the throw. Safe. Gabriel scores.

Puff walks. Logan singles you to third, leaving the bases loaded for Julian.

"Come on, Julian," you shout. "Bring me home!"

Julian knocks the ball high into the air, and you take off for home. But you hear the slap of the ball landing in the third baseman's glove behind you, and you know that the inning is over.

By the third inning, you notice that Gretchen and Mike have arrived. You breathe deep and smile.

Three innings later, the Cardinals lead, 3–1. You're still in right field, ready and waiting.

Just as the batter steps to the plate, you see a police car drive through the parking lot. It's as if you're put into a time machine. You think of the cops finding you, putting your parents in jail, bringing you and your brothers to a stranger's house in the middle of the night.

J.T. must sense your tension. He looks your way, and you lock eyes for a second. He gives you a nod that says, "I understand."

Smack!

The ball flies past J.T. It should have been an easy catch, but he wasn't watching. A Storm runner scores from second base, bringing the score to 3–2. At least there was only one player on base.

They don't score again before the end of the inning. Your team holds on to a one-run lead.

Go to the next page.

As you jog to the dugout, you keep thinking about the police, jail, and your parents. You feel upset. You need something familiar, something you know—like a chance to play at shortstop again. Should you ask Coach Hanson for your position back? Or are you better off staying in the outfield? What will you choose to do?

To ask to play shortstop, go to page 124.

To remain in the outfield, go to page 82.

You can't disappear, but you sure aren't going out to shortstop to humiliate yourself again. You walk over to your coach. "I really messed up this inning. I think J.T. should go back in for me."

"What? You don't think professional baseball players ever mess up?"

"Well, I . . ."

"Of course they do. And do you think they go and ask for a sub?"

"Uh . . . maybe?"

"Maybe? No way. Their coach might take them out, but the players don't make that decision. The real good ones *never* want to come out."

"But, earlier, you asked me to make a decision—"

"That was different. That was for the team. This choice seems like it's all about you. Am I right?"

Yes, he is right. If you give up on the position you love, your family will be very disappointed. You'll be disappointed in yourself, too, if you don't go back to the infield and try again.

You nod. "Sorry I goofed so bad out there. I don't know what happened. I have it sorted out now."

"So get out there and play," Coach replies.

Go to page 117.

You want to win this game. The whole team does. Even J.T. realizes that switching positions gives you the best chance to become state champs. Coach must agree, or he wouldn't be asking.

"J.T. is right," you say. "I'll move over to short."

Coach nods. "Okay, Gibb. Get out there."

You run to your position and settle into your stance. Mike waves at you. Gretchen gives you a thumbs-up. You're thrilled to be back at your spot in the infield.

Your excitement dwindles as Logan walks the first batter. The second batter singles on a soft grounder to third. That puts runners on first and second with nobody out. Your team is already down by a run; you can't afford to let them score again.

Logan bounces back nicely. He strikes out the next batter. That means a double play would end the inning. You find yourself hoping for a ground ball. You could stop the Storm's turn at bat with just one play.

Your wish is granted . . . sort of. The batter screams a ground ball toward you—or, rather, right into the gap between you and Landon at third base.

It's an impossible play, one that you know you can't make. And when the ball passes just out of your reach, the lead runner scores from second base.

That makes it 5–3.

Everything falls apart after that. There's a walk and a hit to right field that J.T. can't get to. Logan's arm finally runs out of energy, and a parade of hits follow. Three, four, five more runners score before Ashton takes over at pitcher.

The Storm bring in another couple of runs before their half inning ends. By then, you're down by nine.

You try to hold onto hope, but the Cardinals' bats stay quiet in the bottom of the ninth. Three outs come too soon. You think about that play you didn't make at shortstop, and you wonder if it was the difference. You also wonder if it's a play that J.T. could have made.

Of course, you'll never know the answer, but it's a question you'll ponder for years to come.

Go to page 75.

You don't want to give your parents a reason to go back to their drugs. You don't even want to give them a headache at this point. Those boys are being jerks, but the best way to avoid trouble is to ignore them.

You turn away, and you pull J.T.'s arm with you. But he snaps it back and quickly pushes the blond kid.

Ugh.

Blondie pushes J.T. in return.

Before the situation can get any worse, you grab J.T.'s waist and try to pull him backward. He shakes you off like a dog drying its wet fur. Then he lunges toward the blond kid and pushes him hard enough to make him fall to the ground.

"Alec!"

You hear your mom's voice, but you don't have time to look at her. Instead, you concentrate on grabbing J.T. again. You have to end this.

"Alec, stop!" she yells.

This time, you fall back with J.T. when he's pushed.

"Knock it off!" your mom screams, but by then, the blond kid is kicking your leg.

You're tangled up with J.T. You can't get out of the way. The only thing you can do is kick blondie off you. You launch your leg toward him—your foot connects squarely with his gut.

He clutches his stomach and drops to the ground. You didn't think you kicked him that hard, but you notice him whimper under his breath.

That's when you hear more voices: men's voices, your coach's voice, a stranger's voice. The fight is over as quickly as it began.

Coach Hanson squeezes your good shoulder as he yanks you and J.T. away from the chaotic scene.

"What were you two thinking?" he barks. "Fighting like that!"

"They started it," you protest.

"Not from where I was sitting," snaps the coach. "I saw J.T. push one of their players, and then I saw you kick him."

"But—"

"Not another word," he interrupts. "I won't have that kind of garbage on my baseball team. You guys are done. Both of you. You're off the team."

Go to page 75.

If your dad is getting into a fight, you don't want to be there. You shut your eyes as tightly as you can and count to ten, pretending you never saw him.

A few minutes later, Mr. Thull parks in front of your house. You hesitate. It's weird to think that you'll go in there and find everything the way you always wanted.

Santana sits atop the couch in the front window, his tail twitching. You take it as a good sign that things inside are normal. You jump out of the car, thank Mr. Thull, and run inside. You smell something incredible.

"Mom?"

"Yeah, in the kitchen."

You throw your backpack down and are about to go in there when you hear August and Andy laughing downstairs. It's the kind of laughter that makes you wonder what they're up to.

You creep downstairs and discover what: They have strung pair after pair of their underwear across the room and are hitting them with a bat as fast as they can, as if the undies were piñatas.

You go back upstairs and to the kitchen, following a scent of something that you can't wait to taste.

You find your mom sitting on the kitchen floor, her phone next to her ear, her free hand pressed against her oddly pale forehead.

"I'll come as soon as I can," she says. She hangs up and stares at nothing in particular.

"What's wrong?" you ask.

"Your dad . . . he got into a fight. He's at the police station right now."

Ugh. You were right.

"Can you please stay with your brothers? I need to get down there." But she doesn't move.

"Is he okay?"

She nods slowly, as tears well in her eyes. "Your dad is okay. The other guy got taken to the hospital." She turns and looks you in the eyes. "Here's the thing, Alec. Dad beat up a guy who used to help us deal. I don't think there will be much trouble, legally. But it means we need to get out of here. It means we need a huge fresh start. Grandma and Aunt Jessy will help, but we'll need to move to Colorado. All of us. Together."

Your smile disappears. "Mom, that means leaving my baseball team."

"I know, and I'm sorry, but it's really the best for our family. You can find another team there. I promise."

Now it's your turn to sit on the kitchen floor. You can't believe it: Your season is over.

Go to page 75.

Right field seems like a good idea. But if you give up on the position you love, your family will be very disappointed. You'll be disappointed in yourself, too, if you don't go back to the infield and try again.

You walk to Coach Hanson. "Sorry I goofed so bad out there. I don't know what happened."

He shrugs.

"I think I have it all sorted out now."

He nods. "So get out there and play."

 AWARD YOURSELF 1 TEAMWORK POINT.

Go to the next page.

You grab your glove and hustle onto the field. You look at Puff. He smiles at you, and you smile back. You punch your glove, bend your knees, and remind yourself that you know how to play this game.

You stay at shortstop until the end, and you play well. J.T. does, too. After trying shortstop and catcher, he finishes the game in right field. Coach mentions that J.T. might become the team's utility player, the person who can fill in at almost any position.

More importantly, your Cardinals win, 6–3.

Afterward, your parents take you and your brothers to Dairy Queen. It has been such an awesome day.

8

School's Out

Spring zips by. The Cardinals' record is an amazing 7–1 when June begins. What seems like all of a sudden, school is out for the summer.

Of course, when it comes to baseball, summer is what the season is all about. You and Puff practice more and more, in between exploring, adventures, and sleepovers. When Puff can't hang out, J.T. usually can. You were worried about him at first, but you're glad he moved here. He's one of your best friends.

Things at home are going well, too. The house is still clean, and your parents are staying out of trouble. Your dad has a job doing cement and rock work. Your mom enters information in the computer, working from home part-time.

June 4 is a game against one of your team's biggest rivals: the Red Earth Rams. Two years ago, they beat you. Last year, you came back to win. They're probably out for a revenge win this year.

The coach starts you at shortstop again. So far, you've started every game but one. J.T. stands by the bench and high-fives the whole team as they rush onto the field. Your dad is working today, but your mom and brothers are in the bleachers.

The first hit floats right to you, and you catch it with ease. Ever since that first game, you've been practicing with Puff, J.T., and also your dad.

Red Earth manages to score a run before the top of the inning is over. Since it's only one, you're sure that your team will come back.

You get a single in the bottom of the inning, but Puff strikes out to end the Cardinals at bat.

Back to the field you go.

The first batter smacks a foul ball that almost hits your brother Andy in the head. Whoa! you hear him say, even this far away from him. "That was cool!"

You shake your head.

The batter works the count to three balls and two strikes. Logan pitches, the batter swings, and something screams directly toward you. It isn't the ball, though.

You'd be ready for that. It takes a moment for your brain to register—the bat.

Just in time, you twist your body so the bat doesn't drill you square in the chest. But you still hear a faint *thunk*. You fall to your knees . . .

You are five years old. Mommy is downstairs, doing laundry. You want to show her the color graph you made in kindergarten today. You're so excited that she's home to show her. She's been gone a lot.

You're paying such close attention to your sheet that you miss the first step. You tumble down the stairs, land just the right way, and snap *goes a bone.*

At the emergency room, you learn that it's a collarbone. Your fingers find it and feel the bump. You have surgery. You wear a sling for six weeks. Each day, the purple fades; the bump is barely there.

A week later, your mom is gone again. Your dad has also disappeared. You and your brothers move in with a foster family. The mom yells a lot; the dad works a lot. The other foster kids hit and kick and throw their food.

Your fingers reach for your collarbone. You don't feel a bump. You didn't hear a snap. How did the bat find the same bone that you broke years ago?

Your heart is knocking on your ribs. You look at the bleachers to see your mom standing, her hands on her hips. Your brothers are standing at the fence behind home plate, gripping the metal, their noses sticking through the diamond-shaped openings. An umpire asks if you're okay, and you say yes.

You climb to your feet before Coach reaches you.

"You okay?" he asks.

No, not really. The pain isn't too bad now, but it feels like it could get worse.

"Yep," you lie. "Just surprised me, that's all."

Your coach looks at you, eye to eye. "You sure?"

You don't want to come out of the game, and you know that's what he's really asking. If you tell him you're fine, he'll let you play. If you say that you're hurt or even that you're worried about your shoulder, he'll sit you on the bench. Your day will be done. Should you play and help your team win? Or is it better to sit out and rest your arm? What will you choose to do?

To tell Coach you're fine, go to page 125.

To tell Coach you're hurt, go to page 142.

You know from experience that covering your ears doesn't work—not even with a pillow. When you hear a *crash*, you jump. You have to get them to stop.

You tiptoe out of your room.

"Don't be so reckless, Brandon!" your mom screams.

"You're the one throwing dishes!" your dad snaps.

"Mom? Dad?" You're halfway down the stairs.

"Alec?" your dad calls. He comes out of the kitchen. "What are you doing down here?"

"Checking on you guys."

He looks down. "Sorry, bud."

Next, your mom appears. "We're so sorry, Alec. Are your brothers awake, too?"

You shrug. "I'm not sure."

She looks at her husband. "We need to go. We're not done talking this out." She grabs her purse and her keys. "Come on, Brandon."

She hurries up the steps and gives you a hug. "We'll be back as soon as we can."

And then they're gone.

When you open your eyes, it's morning. You go down to the kitchen. The place is a total mess: broken pieces of plates on the kitchen floor. In the living room, fluffs of feathers from the couch are sprinkled all around, and it smells worse than Puff's brother after hockey practice. You walk around to the other side of the couch and find a pile of vomit.

You go to the laundry room for supplies: a plastic bag, carpet cleaner, and rags. You don't want your brothers to find the mess.

You must have a strong stomach because you only gag once, and it's cleaned within five minutes. You leave one of the rags covering the wet area and head to the garage to throw away the bag. That's when you find that both of your parents' cars are gone.

Go to page 146.

You think of your parents in jail, and it angers you. You want something normal in your life. You *deserve* it. When you reach the Cardinals' dugout, you go straight to Coach Hanson.

"Coach, I need my position back. Please? It would mean a lot to me."

He shakes his head. "Sorry, Gibb, I need you in right field today. For now, it gives us the best chance to win. If that changes, I'll let you know."

"But Coach—"

He interrupts, "Are you going to do what's best for you or what's best for your teammates?"

You look down and mutter, "Sorry, Coach. I'll do what's best for the team."

Go to page 83.

"Yes, I'm fine," you say. You hate lying, but you hate sitting on the bench even more.

Your coach still stares at you. You force a smile. He slowly turns and walks away, and you exhale. You want to reach up and rub the bone, but you don't. You want to scream as the pain worsens, but you won't.

You pretend to do some warm-ups, focusing on the batter instead of your collarbone.

Logan pitches. The batter swings.

It seems like there should be plenty of time to get out of the ball's path, but there isn't. The baseball smacks you right where the bat did.

You have a moment to wonder, *What are the chances of this happening again?* Then you hear the snap—and you feel the searing pain.

Your last thought is that your season is over, and then you pass out.

Go to page 75.

You've lived your life to play shortstop, and now Coach is taking it away from you—after your parents got thrown into jail! You're not going to deal with this drama anymore. You'll quit the team.

You pack up your stuff and wait for Puff to come off the field. His dad will take you back to Caren and Eddie's place.

"I'm so excited for tomorrow's game," Puff says.

You don't respond.

"Aren't you?"

"I quit. Coach moved me to right field, and J.T. gets to play my position."

"Oh, man . . . but you can't quit."

"I just did."

Puff tries to change your mind. Some of the other players do, too. But you refuse to listen. Your mind is made up.

The Cardinals might win the state championship, or they might not. Either way, they'll do it without you. Your days of playing for Coach Hanson are at an end.

Go to page 75.

It's weird, but some moments in life seem to slow down, as if you're living in slow motion. Each detail moves through space and time so clearly and precisely.

Of course, in reality, you run as if you're being chased by a hungry tiger. Then you try to repeat exactly what J.T. did, diving through the air and making your arms grow long.

You feel the baseball hit the tip of your glove, and you squeeze your hand together. The baseball rolls into your webbing, and it sticks.

You land hard, feeling a slight jar against your collarbone. But your elation at catching the ball quickly makes you forget the sting.

"Great catch!" Julian exclaims next to you. "Are you okay, Gibb?"

You look at him, and a smile stretches across your face. "I'm awesome. Now, let's go win this game!"

As Julian helps you up, the rest of the Cardinals run to the dugout. Thanks to your spectacular catch, the championship is still within reach.

Go to the next page.

The Cardinals start the bottom half of the ninth at the top of your batting order.

"Come on, Ben," you yell. "Hit the moon!"

He strikes out.

Gabriel steps to the plate. When he swings, the ball soars deep to right field. You leap to your feet. You watch as it keeps going and going. The outfielder runs back, back, back.

The ball lands in the outfielder's glove.

Crud.

The championship falls to Ashton, and it's as if none of your teammates know how to breathe. Everyone seems completely still.

The silence is broken by the *thunk* of Ashton's bat hitting the ball. The baseball zooms over second base and bounces in front of the center fielder. Ashton hustles to first base.

Now, it's your turn. Although you try to talk yourself out of being nervous, you feel like you could puke. Right here, right now. You're pretty sure that you've never felt this nervous before in your life. However, the very moment you step inside the batter's box, a sudden sense of calm washes over you.

You swing your bat to loosen your shoulders.

"Come on, Alec!" Mike shouts. "Let's go!"

The pitcher throws; you swing . . . and miss.

You step out of the box and practice your swing. Thoughts of last year's failure try to creep into your mind, but you push them away. That was another time, and you're a better player—a better person—now.

The next pitch is too high. You foul off the pitch after that. Strike two.

"Come on now, Gibb!" Coach shouts.

You take a deep breath. This moment is going to take everything you have—everything you've worked so hard to become.

Add together all of your points.

If you have 12 or more points, go to page 152.

If you have 11 or fewer points, go to page 74.

You made a good decision: You took yourself out of the game. That was courageous, not quitting. These guys have nothing on you. You bet they've never broken their collarbones. You bet they live in nice little houses with parents who aren't drug addicts. You bet they've never had to go to another family's house in the middle of the night.

These two aren't worth getting in trouble for, but you won't let J.T. get in trouble for you, either. So it's up to you to act first. You take the ice pack in your hand and swing it into the blond's shoulder.

His face flushes red. He glares at you and clenches his fists. He looks ready to pounce.

That's when you hear your mom's voice.

"Well, hi, boys! It's so nice of you to catch up after the game." She puts her hand on your back. "You know what's strange, though?" she continues. "I think you're arguing. Am I right?"

None of you answer.

"Now, Alec, I've told you before that I make good cookies, but they're certainly not the best. So please don't argue over whose mama has the best chocolate chip cookies. Okay?"

She moves between you and the other boys, and you turn and head straight to the car.

She doesn't talk the entire drive. But as soon as you get home, she follows you into the living room. "Sit."

You do.

"I saw that stunt with the ice pack back there."

You don't answer.

"What were you going to do to those boys?"

You look down at your glove in your lap.

"From what I saw, I think you were going to fight. Is that correct?"

You shake your head, just barely.

"That would've been a very bad choice."

"Look who's talking," you mumble.

"Excuse me?"

You look up, but you don't repeat yourself.

"Alec, you have no idea how many times I chant that in my head when I'm sitting in a cell. 'You made a bad choice again.' But this addiction is so strong." She runs her hands through her hair. "Your dad and I are trying to fight it. And we're *trying* to be parents to you three boys. With that said, you're grounded for a week. Don't ever even think about hitting someone."

At first, you're ticked. But it's not like you can do much, anyway, not with your hurt collarbone.

"Go wash up. We need to find something to eat."

9

State Semifinals

It's August 2: the day of the state semifinals. Your team hasn't lost since June. The Cardinals have again proven to be one of the strongest squads in the state.

Your collarbone has been perfectly fine for weeks. In fact, it didn't affect your season in the least. J.T. came in to play shortstop every once in awhile, but you didn't miss a single game. Plus, as your collarbone has gotten stronger, so has your team. You won the quarterfinal game by blowing out the Northfield Eagles, 11–2.

Instead of talking baseball, though, your brothers talk nonstop about school. You'd never admit it to them, but you're nervous about going back in a few weeks. You really liked Mrs. Rogers.

As you get ready for today's game, you try not to think about last night's dinner, how your mom and dad didn't talk. Andy and August talked. You just listened to your parents' silence and watched them move their food around without really eating.

You finally asked, "Are you coming to my game?"

"Yep," your dad answered. "Puff's dad asked if we could drive Puff. I'll pick him up after my shift."

You're not sure if your dad still actually works. Sometimes he comes home mid-morning. Your mom doesn't seem to work as much, either. Sure, she slips into her desk chair in the mornings. But you see her walking up and down the stairs every hour or so, for about 10 minutes each time, sometimes holding a coffee, sometimes playing with her hair. Up and down. More often lately, though, she just walks up and down like a zombie.

You pick up Puff at 4 p.m. and ride toward the city. You and Puff talk about the camping trip you'll take after the baseball season ends, before school begins.

When your dad parks the car at the field, he turns to the backseat. "Andy, August, go with your brother. Mom and I have to talk."

You feel a knot in your stomach. "Dad, I have to warm up."

"Yes, I know. Just get them to the bleachers. They'll sit there." His eyes dart back and forth between your brothers. "You *will* sit there and wait for us."

"Okay," says August.

"Okay," mimics Andy.

After escorting your brothers, you hurry onto the field. Your body feels great. You just need to turn off your racing mind.

Today, you're playing the Edina Silver, a team from a city that's about six times bigger than yours. They've been highly ranked for several years in a row, but your team won't be intimidated by that. Coach Hanson has told you over and over, "We have the talent, boys. Don't let a big team from a big city scare you. You're a good team, just like they are. Now, let's fire it up!"

Ben starts the Cardinals off with a single. Gabriel repeats the play. Ashton, however, strikes out, leaving runners at first and second base.

You're up. You see two balls and two strikes before you hit a liner down the alley in left center. Ben makes it home, scoring your only run of the inning.

After you get to your position at shortstop, you look up at the bleachers. You don't see your mom. Your dad isn't looking at you—or anyone on the team. He seems to be staring off, past the outfield. You're so distracted that you miss the first pitch: a hit that zooms past you on the left. The batter hustles around to second base.

"All right, now," Puff says, "let's go, Cardinals."

Then you see your mom. She's sitting on the hood of your dad's Camaro, knees pulled up, arms wrapped around herself as tight as a baseball stitch. You're not sure from this far away, but you think she's crying—and she's shaking.

"Gibb!" Landon yells.

You turn toward his voice, but now he's looking past you. When you spin around, the ball is being thrown to him. Landon chucks the ball to Ben at home plate, but the runner is safe. You totally messed up another play.

You need to get your head in the game, but can you do that if you're worried about your Mom? You want to go and check on her, but that means you'll be done for the rest of the game—the state semifinals. Will you go to your mom and check on her, or will you stay in the game? What will you choose to do?

To check on your mom, go to page 78.

To stay in the game, go to page 140.

"Coach," you say, "are you asking me to decide?"

"Yes, Gibb, I am. It's your choice."

On the one hand, you think the coach should make the decision. He is the coach, after all. On the other hand, you like knowing that he trusts you.

You've gotten to know J.T. pretty well, and he's a good friend. But this is the first game, and you want to finish it. Besides, he might be better than you—so you don't want to lose your starting position.

"I'd rather stay in, Coach. I've had a good game, so I just want to keep going."

"Fine by me," he answers.

You run to your spot between second base and third base, punch your fist into your glove, and bend your knees. Logan throws a pitch. The batter swings. There's a loud *crack*—and you barely have time to register the ball speeding straight at your face . . .

You wake up in the hospital. Your whole body feels as heavy as a set of bleachers. It hurts to open your eyes, like the skin on your face is being pulled over the top of your head. When you try to talk, a new pain shoots into your brain and down your neck.

Gingerly, you reach up and touch your face—parts are covered with bandages. You feel a few stitches, too.

But the right side of your face is the weirdest. It's bumpy, and it's metal, as if a coat hanger has been stuffed into your mouth.

What happened?

You don't have to wait long for an answer. When a nurse comes to check on you, she explains how the line drive shattered your cheekbone. It gave you a massive concussion, too. The damage is so bad, in fact, that the doctor isn't sure if you'll ever play baseball again.

Go to page 75.

It's weird, but some moments in life seem to slow down, as if you're living in slow motion. Each detail moves through space and time so clearly and precisely.

Of course, in reality, you run as if you're being chased by a hungry tiger. Then you try to repeat exactly what J.T. did, diving through the air and making your arms grow long.

You feel the baseball hit the tip of your glove, and you land hard, feeling a slight jar against your collarbone. Then you see the ball bounce to the ground and dribble away from you.

You missed it.

You look to your left, and Julian scrambles for the still rolling ball. You spin to your right to see one—then two—runners cross home plate.

Julian throws the ball to the infield, and the rest of the base runners stop. But the damage is done.

Logan's arm finally runs out of energy, and a parade of hits follow. One, two, three runners score before Ashton takes over at pitcher.

The Storm bring in another couple of runs before their half inning ends. By then, you're behind by eight.

You try to hold onto hope, but the Cardinals go down quietly in the bottom of the ninth. You think about that play you didn't make, and you wonder if it was the difference. Of course, you'll never know the answer, but it's a question that you'll ponder for years to come.

Go to page 75.

Your mom seems upset—but not hurt. She'll be fine. Plus, she knows how important this game is and will be mad if you leave it to check on her. You shift your eyes from your mom to the batter.

Logan hurls a ball right into Ben's glove. Strike.

Your eyes shift to Mom again. She's still crying.

Crud. You need to stop looking at her. You face the batter . . . eyes back to your mom . . . back to the batter. *Knock it off. Stop being so distracted.*

There's a loud *crack*—and you barely have time to register the ball speeding straight at your face . . .

You wake up in the hospital. Your whole body feels as heavy as a set of bleachers. It hurts to open your eyes, like the skin on your face is being pulled over the top of your head. When you try to talk, a new pain shoots into your brain and down your neck.

Gingerly, you reach up and touch your face—parts are covered with bandages. You feel a few stitches, too. But the right side of your face is the weirdest. It's bumpy, and it's metal, as if a coat hanger has been stuffed into your mouth.

What happened?

You don't have to wait long for an answer. When a nurse comes to check on you, she explains how the line drive shattered your cheekbone. It gave you a massive concussion, too. The damage is so bad, in fact, that the doctor isn't sure if you'll ever play baseball again.

Go to page 75.

"No," you say, gritting your teeth. "I guess I'm not okay. I broke my collarbone when I was little, and the doctor always told me . . ."

Coach Hanson nods. "You're a smart kid. You know when to buck up and when to bow out." He walks you back to the bench.

J.T. rushes to your side. "Dude, you okay?"

"I think so. It didn't break."

"J.T.," Coach says, "I need you at shortstop."

"Okay," he replies over his shoulder. He looks at you and smiles. "We still got a lot of summer to ride bikes."

"Right," you say.

J.T. runs onto the field.

 AWARD YOURSELF 1 CONFIDENCE POINT.

"Alec," your mom calls from behind the fence.

You go to her.

"Did it—" she asks.

"Nah, it didn't break."

"I'll get some ice for it."

She's so concerned; she wants to take care of you. You wish she'd take better care of herself. She doesn't eat enough, these days. She's let her hair go, too. She barely bothers to clean herself up anymore.

She's back with an ice pack in no time. "Do you want to head home?" she asks.

"No, I'll stay and watch the game."

"Okay, I'll be in the bleachers."

When you sit down and rest the pack against your bone, you imagine how it could always be this way: your mom with you, helping you, acting like a mom. But you've seen things turn so quickly in the past, and your mind isn't ready to give up on that possibility.

The game ends with a score of 5–2; the Cardinals win again. The coach compliments the team and tells you what you'll be working on in practice, and then he dismisses everyone.

"Alec," Coach says, "stay out of trouble." He winks and walks away.

Your mom and brothers are already in the car, but as you walk toward the parking lot with J.I., a couple of the Red Earth players fall in step behind you.

"Hey, chicken, hurt your wing?" the blond one says.

"What a wimp," laughs the other.

The first adds, "Seriously, I've been hit in the head and still played the rest of the game."

"Loser," snaps the other.

You turn. "You guys lost the game, not us."

"Yeah, sure, we lost," says the blond, "but at least we didn't quit."

You see J.T.'s fists clench. He looks ready to attack. He whispers to you, "Do something, or I will."

If you start a fight, you'll get into big trouble. If you don't do anything, J.T. might get into trouble for you. You can ignore those two and walk away. Maybe that will be the end of it. Or perhaps you can cool J.T.'s nerves—and your own—by nudging the blond one with your ice pack. J.T. would probably laugh at that, rather than start a fight. What will you choose to do?

To ignore them, go to page 112.

To nudge them with an ice pack, go to page 130.

They're yelling so loudly. If you go out there, you'll just make it worse. Instead, you cover your head with your pillow and try to stifle the angry sounds.

It does little good, so you snap on your reading light and open a book. Maybe you can escape into another world and stop hearing your parents destroy yours.

When you open your eyes, it's morning. Your book is skewed on your bed, your bookmark on the floor, your reading light still on. You hear silence. You open your door and dare to go down the stairs to the kitchen.

The place is a total mess: broken pieces of plates on the kitchen floor. In the living room, fluffs of feathers from the couch are sprinkled all around, and it smells worse than Puff's brother after hockey practice. You walk around to the other side of the couch and find a pile of vomit.

You go to the laundry room for supplies: a plastic bag, carpet cleaner, and rags. You don't want your brothers to find the mess.

You must have a strong stomach because you only gag once, and it's cleaned within five minutes. You leave one of the rags covering the wet area and head to the garage to throw away the bag. That's when you find that both of your parents' cars are gone.

Back inside, you hear your brothers. You go to their room. They're playing on the iPad.

"Special treat today: pancakes in bed," you say.

"Yay!" they both yell.

"But you guys need to stay here, okay?"

"Duh," says August. "How can we have breakfast in bed if we're on the couch?"

"Good point," you say and shut the door.

At 3 p.m., your parents still aren't home. On the one hand, you should be worried. On the other, you don't need to worry because they've done this before.

You call Puff and ask if his sister can babysit while you go to practice. "It's kind of an emergency," you say. "I don't know where my parents are."

Puff's sister comes. Puff's dad drives you to practice. He doesn't ask if everything is okay; he probably knows it's not. You smile at Puff to let him know how much you appreciate his support.

Practice is one of your worst ever. You drop fly balls, miss ground balls, throw balls everywhere except where you want them to go. Even your legs don't seem to work. You trip and fall on at least three occasions. This is not a good sign before the championship game.

When you get home, your parents are still gone.

After an evening filled with "Where's Mom?" and "Where's Dad?" you finally get your brothers into bed. You're almost ready to call Gretchen and Mike when you hear the garage door open.

You wait in your bedroom, hoping your parents will come in to explain themselves—or at least to say good night. A minute passes. Then two. Three.

You leave your room and are about to head downstairs when you see your parents' bedroom door. You didn't hear it, but it's shut. You put your ear against the door but don't hear anything inside.

You don't get very much sleep that night. You keep waking up, thinking you've missed the beginning of the championship game. Your dreams are just quick blips of baseball and cars and your parents.

10

Out of Position

Practice goes much better on Wednesday, probably because things seem more normal with your parents. They got up before you and your brothers and made breakfast, and your mom sat at her desk in the living room. Your dad left. Maybe they both found new jobs.

Thursday, you don't see your parents all day, just a closed bedroom door. At practice, Coach Hanson has you playing pickle. This gives you a thrill, and you get more excited about the big game on Saturday.

Some time in the middle of the night, you hear a knock on your door. You think you're dreaming and ignore it. But then it sounds again, louder.

You sit up and rub your eyes.

The door opens, and you see a strange silhouette against the hallway light.

"Hello, Alec? It's Officer Keith. Remember me from last spring?"

It takes a moment to register, but eventually you do remember him. You nod, although you're not sure if he sees it in the darkness of your room.

He continues, "I need to take you and your brothers to emergency foster care."

The words hit you like a slap in the face. You start to cry. How can this be happening *again*? A million other questions swirl around in your head. You only muster enough strength to ask, "Why?"

Officer Keith sits on the edge of your bed. "Sorry to tell you, but they were selling prescription medication again. They were taking some, too."

Your fingers rub your collarbone, and you sob. You haven't cried this hard since that day in school. But you can't help it. What's going to happen to your family?

You pack some clothes and your baseball gear. You find your brothers waiting in the living room with Officer Ellers, although it looks like Andy is asleep.

Since Mike and Gretchen are on a vacation, the officers take you to an emergency foster care family, one you haven't visited before. They let you into their

149

home without much to say. You three go into the same room. Andy crawls into bed with you and cries himself back to sleep.

These foster parents, Caren and Eddie Jackson, are quiet, but they get you to practice on Friday. It's another bad day for you. You can't focus. Your parents are in jail, and there's nothing you can do about it.

Coach calls you over to the bench halfway through practice. "What's going on, Gibb?"

"My parents. They're in jail again."

He grimaces. "Sorry to hear that."

You look down and kick the ground. "Me, too."

"I have an idea," says Coach, "one that might ease your mind a bit. I'm thinking of putting you in right field for the championship."

Your mouth drops open.

"I want you in the lineup. You're a strong play—"

"But not as strong as J.T. at shortstop?" Your voice sounds angrier than you intended.

"Right now, to ease your mind, playing right field will be the best thing."

"I think playing my position is the best thing."

"Gibb, I'm not going to argue with you about this. You have a lot on your mind right now."

"But taking my position from me isn't helping."

Coach shrugs. "Sorry you disagree. You can play right field or sit on the bench." He walks away before you can respond.

How many confidence points do you have?

If you have three or more points, go to page 102.

If you have two or fewer points, go to page 126.

You step out of the box again to practice your swing. You don't mean for it to happen—and you sure don't want it to—but thoughts of your parents sneak into your mind. These are the parents of long ago, the ones who spent time with you at the baseball field, who cheered you on as you learned the sport. These are your parents who starred in softball and baseball. These are your parents who are *not* users or sellers . . . or criminals.

You shake away the thoughts and step back in.

The pitcher winds up . . .

Your parents do *try for you.*

The ball hurtles toward you . . .

Your parents do *care for you.*

You swing with all of your might . . .

Your parents do *love you.*

You feel the familiar *twang* in your hands, and you see the ball shoot back the way it came. You know that you hit it well, but there's no time to admire it. You catch a glimpse of the baseball drifting toward the gap between the center fielder and the right fielder.

The hit is deep enough to be a double for sure, but you're smart. You know what the outfielders are going to do. You immediately tell yourself, *Get to third base.*

Your hunch is correct. The right fielder grabs the ball and chucks it toward home plate—instead of toward third base—so you stroll onto third without even needing to slide.

You spin to watch the play at home plate, but there really isn't one. You hit the ball so deeply—and Ashton was running so fast—that he makes it home well ahead of the baseball. He slides, just in case, and the umpire signals, "Safe!"

You clap your hands together one time, and then you pump your fist in the air. You did it. You came through. The game is tied.

Now, it's up to Puff.

Your best friend watches a couple of pitches for balls but also swings and misses twice. The Storm's pitcher is wearing down, though, just like Logan was. He uses his jersey to wipe the sweat off his face. Then he winds up and flings a fastball straight toward the catcher's mitt.

The ball never gets there. It bounces off the ground in front of home plate, hits the catcher, and ricochets off the umpire's shoulder.

For a moment, no one knows where the baseball is. No one except for you. You see it on the grass between the pitcher's mound and home plate. It bounced back in that direction.

In a split second, you decide to risk it. You sprint toward home plate.

The catcher points, yells, crouches, and readies his glove. You rush forward with one final burst of energy, and then you slide.

There's a moment of chaos. You feel home plate; you feel the catcher's mitt tag you. But which came first?

You roll onto your stomach and look up toward the umpire. He nods and his arms fly out like wings—and you know that you're safe! Safe at home!

You jump off the ground. Puff hugs you, lifts you, squeezes you. Then J.T.'s there. Ashton. Logan. Everyone. Someone hops on top of you, and you all fall to the ground, laughing, screaming, flying.

The Cardinals are state champions!

Epilogue

You and your brothers begin the school year living with your grandma in Colorado. But everyone agrees it's temporary. There's talk that you'll move home again by Christmas.

The championship game seemed to spark something inside your parents. No one knows why it had such an impact on them—maybe because you were the hero, and they missed it. But your mom and dad are working harder than ever before to get well. They've even gone into rehab and have started to get counseling.

Your time in Colorado will be fine; you'll probably make plenty of new friends. But you can't wait to get back to Chane Valley. You and your teammates have a championship to defend.

YOU WIN

Congratulations!

CHOOSE TO WIN!

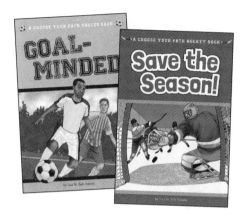

Read the fast-paced, action-packed stories. Make the right choices. Find your way to the "winning" ending!

Goal-Minded
Out at Home
Save the Season

YOU'RE THE MAIN CHARACTER. YOU MAKE THE CHOICES.

CAN YOU SURVIVE?

20,000 Leagues Under the Sea
Adventures of Perseus
Adventures of Sherlock Holmes
Call of the Wild
Dracula
King Solomon's Mines
Merry Adventures of Robin Hood
Three Musketeers
Treasure Island
Twelve Labors of Hercules

About the Author

Lisa M. Bolt Simons has been a teacher for more than 20 years, and she's been a writer for as long as she can remember. She has written more than 20 nonfiction children's books, as well as a history book, *Faribault Woolen Mill: Loomed in the Land of Lakes*, and she is currently working on several other projects. Both her nonfiction and fiction works have been recognized with various accolades.

In her spare time, Lisa loves to read and to scrapbook. Originally from Colorado, Lisa currently lives in Minnesota with her husband, Dave, and she's the mom of twins, Jeri and Anthony. She was a busy sports mom for over a decade.

CONFIDENCE:

SKILL:

SPEED:

TEAMWORK:

TALENT POINTS:

CONFIDENCE:

SKILL:

SPEED:

TEAMWORK:

TALENT POINTS:

CONFIDENCE:

SKILL:

SPEED:

TEAMWORK:

TALENT POINTS: